IN LOVE WITH A RAKE

Oliver moved near the fire, and Emily joined him there. When his gaze met hers, time seemed to stand still. There was a magnetism in his blue eyes that sent her senses reeling. Their mesmerized gazes remained locked, and the only sound in the room was the cracking of the fire. The muted conversation of passing servants in the hall seemed to bring the earl from his trance, but there was a huskiness in his voice. "I merely wanted to thank you for what you did in protecting my nephew."

As every nerve in her body seemed to tingle at his look, Emily struggled to keep her thoughts on the conversation. "My lord, I hope you are not too disappointed to discover Lady Cora's shortcomings."

Oliver was amazed at the depth of his feelings for the woman before him. He struggled to keep his desire for Emily in check. He wanted to crush her to him and devour her, but she was not some practiced mistress, only an innocent in the ways of love. Instead he gave in to impulse only to the extent of tracing his finger along her jawline before lifting her chin. "I discovered a great deal more than that today, my dear."

Emily's heart raced as she took his meaning; then the earl's mouth covered hers. She knew she should be outraged that he'd taken such a liberty, but instead she surrendered herself freely to the passion in his kiss. She'd tried to keep from falling victim to his charms, but when his lips touched hers, she knew she was lost. She was in love with Oliver Carson. . . .

D1400623

Books by Lynn Collum

A GAME OF CHANCE
ELIZABETH AND THE MAJOR
THE SPY'S BRIDE
LADY MIRANDA'S MASQUERADE
AN UNLIKELY FATHER

Published by Zebra Books

AN UNLIKELY FATHER

Lynn Collum

Zebra Books
Kensington Publishing Corp.
http://www.zebrabooks.com

ZEBRA BOOKS are published by

Kensington Publishing Corp.
850 Third Avenue
New York, NY 10022

Copyright © 1999 by Jerry Lynn Smith

All rights reserved. No part of this book may be reproduced
in any form or by any means without the prior written consent
of the Publisher, excepting brief quotes used in reviews.

If you purchased this book without a cover you should be
aware that this book is stolen property. It was reported as "un-
sold and destroyed" to the Publisher and neither the Author
nor the Publisher has received any payment for this "stripped
book."

Zebra and the Z logo Reg. U.S. Pat. & TM Off.

First Printing: November, 1999
10 9 8 7 6 5 4 3 2 1

Printed in the United States of America

One

India—1813

The white lattice door opened, and a pretty young woman stepped into the large sitting room of the suite in the Royal Arms Inn. This largest hotel in Calcutta, with its Chippendale furniture and Aubusson rugs, provided newly arrived and soon-to-depart British travelers with accommodations both elegant and reminiscent of home. Yet the large room also held touches of the local ambience in its paintings of tiger hunts and exotic statues of Hindustani deities as well as the finest sheer Indian muslins billowing at the open windows.

The young lady, long accustomed to the odd mixture of cultures in the decor, waited for the sitting room's other occupant to take note of her. Unfortunately, Mrs. Delia Keaton, her blond head bowed, was so engrossed in a book that she paid scant attention to the small disruption to her solitude.

Miss Emily Collins cleared her throat and placed her hands upon her slender hips. "Whatever are you reading that is so interesting?"

The beginnings of a smile tipped Delia's mouth as she closed the book, but her features froze when she looked up and took in her employer's attire. "Emily Collins!" Mrs. Keaton cried incredulously. "I thought you had gone shopping for new gowns for the journey home, not for one of those indecent costumes."

"Do you not think it pretty?" Emily twirled about in the traditional red wedding *sari* ornately worked with patterns of gold. The thin garment's skirt flared, exposing bare ringed feet and slender ankles.

Delia could only shake her head in amazement. There was no denying that Emily looked a vision in the exotic costume, with her light brown hair loose and curling beneath the sheer red veil. A single gold fob, resting on her forehead, dangled from a chain which held the headdress in place. But no decent Englishwoman would expose her stomach as Emily now did. The Indian dress consisted of a red *choli,* a small, short-sleeved bodice, which covered the bosom, and below a bared abdomen, a snug underskirt of red silk molded to narrow hips over which the red and gold muslin *sari* was draped, then drawn up over the shoulder, falling behind like a cape. The whole effect was scandalous in the young widow's view.

"My dear, you cannot think to wear anything so . . . so shocking once we are in London. You would be given the cut direct by all of Society if you appeared thus in public, even at a costume ball."

"Are you certain? If the manner in which people treat me in Calcutta since I inherited my uncle's wealth is any indication, then I could wear this costume while riding an elephant with a monkey atop my head in Hyde Park and still be welcomed at the fashionable parties." Emily was referring to the fact that until six months before she'd often been treated as a poor relation during her trips to the British seat of power in India. This time, with her uncle dead and his flourishing estate near Murshidabad sold, she had been treated as the much-feted heiress by many of the gentlemen employed by the East India Company.

Delia laughed, then sobered. "Ah, so upon your return to London you intend to establish the reputation of being the Eccentric Miss Collins. Well, just remember that a swain has no say in your conduct, but a husband is quite another matter. Married, your eccentricity would suddenly become madness. You would likely find yourself locked in an attic in a country estate, your imaginary monkey and elephant sent to dreadful cages in Town."

Emily eyed her companion closely. It had taken the better part of a year to hear the story of the cruel Major Keaton from the shy Delia. Her views on the nature of some men were well known to Emily, and there was no reason to speak of such dark matters. Instead, she teased her friend, "Then should I cancel the order for a monkey and an elephant to be delivered to the ship tomorrow?"

Surprise raced across Delia Keaton's face; then, recognizing the mischievous twinkle in Emily's eyes, she shook her head and smiled. "Only promise me you will not wear that costume in company once we begin to go about in Society."

Emily walked over to her friend and gave her a hug. "Have no fear, dear Delia. I bought it merely to wear in the privacy of my bedchamber when I become homesick for my Calcutta."

A pensive look settled on Emily's face as her gaze trailed to the view from the window. She'd lived in the Bengal Province nearly fifteen years, first with her uncle and aunt, a lady who'd found the climate not to her liking. Then, after Aunt Olivia's death, Delia had joined the household as Emily's companion.

Unlike most who came out to make their fortunes, Emily considered England the foreign world and India her home. She turned and walked through the peaked-arch doors onto the balcony, the vista of Calcutta spreading out in front of her.

Delia rose and followed, despite her dislike of the heat and exotic smells of the nearby street markets. Worry lines were etched into her pretty face as she came to stand beside her friend and employer. There could be little doubt in her mind that Emily was nervous about her return to the land of her birth. One always feared the unknown, and that was what awaited the young heiress in England.

The widow grasped the stone balustrade, but remained quiet, since Emily appeared lost in memories as she stood in almost a trance-like state. The noise from the street drifted upwards, but the ladies had long grown familiar with the busy streets of the town.

The prospect from the balcony covered the green fields surrounding Fort William and the muddy Hughli River beyond. The British military fortress represented stability in a land where little remained constant as the *nawabs* and *rajahs* struggled against each other and the British Army for control of the bountiful East India trade.

At last, with a sigh, Emily broke the silence. "I have heard many tales of life in London. I am certain I shall enjoy the plays and museums, but I don't know if I wish to enter Society and waste my days in making calls and other idle pursuits among strangers."

Delia placed a hand on Emily's exposed arm. "You

will think differently once you are welcomed home by all your English relations."

A bitter laugh escaped Emily's lips. "Oh, I am certain they will welcome the heiress from the East Indies, even though none would house the penniless orphan from Warwickshire all those years ago."

Emily had been but ten years old when her parents were killed in a carriage accident. At the funeral there had been numerous consultations of family members behind closed doors at her uncle's estate near Coventry, the result of which was that her father's only brother was unwilling to take and raise a child with no income. It had fallen to her mother's younger brother, Mr. Nathaniel Ashton, then about to embark to Calcutta to make his fortune with his new wife, to take young Emily with them.

Delia was unable to defend the actions of people she didn't know, so she had no answer for her friend. She fell silent. As the destitute widow of an army officer, Delia had been subjected to much of the same rejection and humiliation as Emily by Calcutta's English community. But Mr. Ashton had also come to the young widow's rescue with an offer to become companion to his niece, and her life was now one of comfort and ease.

In the distance, the sound of a lone male voice echoed in the hot June air. The warbling singsong cry called the small sect of faithful Muslims to evening prayers. It was a familiar sound in this land of many religions, but still it jarred both women out of their private thoughts.

Delia avoided looking at the shocking red gown; instead, she gazed into Emily's amber eyes. "You may want to change. You will scandalize Swarup when he brings our tea."

Emily nodded, then sighed. "I cannot believe this will be my last night in Calcutta." With that she left her companion and returned to her bedchamber.

Delia remained some minutes on the balcony taking one last look at the British fort, the source of the so-called Black Hole of Calcutta. She'd been a frightened bride in a loveless marriage on her arrival in Bengal three years ago. She pushed thoughts of that time from her mind. Her memories of Calcutta were not so pleasant as Emily's, and she would have few regrets when the ship sailed for England on the morrow.

A knock sounded on the sitting room door. Delia entered the room as she patted her lace cap, making certain it was in place, and called for the visitor to enter. Swarup, the Indian servant, slipped quietly in, as was his habit, but to Delia's surprise he carried no tea tray. He bowed very formally.

The Indian was of indeterminate age and large in stature, which gave him a menacing appearance. But Delia had never met a man whose nature was as gentle as the young giant's. His plain white attire included an intricately wrapped turban on his head, making his skin appear dark brown. *"Memsahib,* there is an Englishman here to see Miss Emily. He says it is very urgent."

Delia's gaze drifted to the door through which Emily had disappeared. Dare she risk inviting the unknown visitor to come up, not knowing if Emily had returned to proper attire? But she could not leave the gentleman cooling his heels in the lobby of the hotel. "Send him up, Swarup, and hold our tea until Miss Collins calls for you."

Delia hurried to warn Emily of their impending visitor and was relieved to find her friend once again suitably dressed in a simple lavender muslin gown with black ribbons. It was as close as she'd gotten to mourning colors, her uncle having stipulated that she not drape herself in black. She promised to join Delia and their guest once her brown curls were again neatly secured.

Within minutes, a tall gentleman with gaunt features, piercing blue eyes and thinning red hair entered the sitting room to greet Delia. There was nothing fashionable about him; the collar of his shirt was neither high nor starched, and his black coat seemed cut more for comfort than style. He bowed and introduced himself as Mr. Hamilton Avery, Solicitor.

Delia gestured for him to come to a seat near her. "Good afternoon, sir. I am Mrs. Keaton, Miss Collins's companion. She will join us in a moment."

When Emily arrived, Mr. Avery rose and immediately launched into the reason for his intrusion, his face a study of concern. "Miss Collins, no doubt you have heard of Mr. James Carson."

Emily wrinkled her brow in thought as she took a seat. Calcutta was a community some hundred thousand strong, but, as in England, the elite moved in what constituted Society at Mrs. Hastings's assembly rooms and the Chowringhee Theatre. Emily's acquaintances in the Quality were numerous. "Does he own an indigo plantation near Haora?"

The solicitor's face relaxed a bit as he again settled into his chair. "He does."

"I fear, Mr. Avery, I know little about the gentleman other than that. I don't believe he comes into Calcutta very often."

The gentleman glanced down at his hands for a moment, then looked back at Miss Collins. "He has had little luck since coming to the Indies to make his fortune. I fear that in the past year what luck he's had has all been bad. His wife died in childbirth last year, and now he lies near death at his estate from the fever."

Delia and Emily exchanged a sad and knowing look. The unfortunate fact of life in this part of the world was that the mortality rate always ran high, especially during the long months of the hot Indian summer.

Mr. Avery continued before either lady could comment. "That is the reason I have come to you. Mr. Carson has begged me to find someone to return his motherless children to their uncle, who resides near Bath, and I learned at the docks that you are to depart for England in the morning."

Emily's doubts seemed to be reflected on her face as her finely drawn brows drew downward. "Sir, I cannot think that Mr. Carson would wish a complete stranger to take charge of his children. Should he not ask some acquaintance to—"

"I fear that the gentleman may never recover, Miss Collins, and I think that is in his mind as well. He wants to know that the children are safely on their way to England before the monsoons begin. Otherwise they may be stranded at the plantation for months with no one but servants to see to them, should the worst occur."

The torrential rains which plagued the region from June until August were due any day. If the Carson family lost their father, goodness knew what would happen to them during the long months of isolation. How could she, an unwanted orphan in her youth, abandon them in the heart of Bengal? Emily knew she had little choice but to aid Mr. Carson in returning his children to his brother.

"Sir, I shall take the children to their uncle, but my ship sails in the morning. How will you get them here in time?"

Mr. Avery's face puckered into what could only be called a smile for all its tortured appearance. "I was certain you would agree, miss. I have them in the Carsons' carriage down below. I assure you they will be no trouble, for they have their nurse with them." He reached into his pocket and drew out a packet of documents. "The one on top is for you. It is the Earl of Hawksworth's direction and funds to compensate you for the children's expenses. The other papers are letters for the children's uncle."

Emily glanced at her companion as she took the packet, but her friend's face was an unreadable mask. Perhaps Delia thought her employer was being impetuous to be taking on such a responsibility, but the shy companion offered Emily no rebuke. "Delia, please summon Swarup and arrange for rooms for the addition to our party and send word to Captain Blackmon of the change in our needs as well."

With that, Emily looked to Mr. Avery. "Shall we bring the children inside, sir?"

The young heiress followed the solicitor downstairs and out into the street in front of the hotel. A huge, ancient traveling carriage weathered by the hot tropical sun stood surrounded by a crowd of dirty street urchins. Mr. Avery shooed away the gawkers, then signaled to one of the brown-skinned servants, and the door was opened to reveal an astonishing sight.

Crammed into the carriage were three children. An infant was sleeping in the arms of an *ayah,* an Indian nurse, whose eyes reflected fear, although of what Emily could not be certain. There was also a little girl of perhaps five and a young lad of six or seven seated on the opposite bench. Most startling, however, was that the small space also included a goat, an oversized birdcage with two large parrots—one red, one green—and a tiny black dog of mysterious lineage who was sniffing the goat as if he'd found his next meal.

Emily's hand fluttered to her mouth even as her stomach plummeted. "Surely you cannot mean for me to travel with this collection of animals as well as the children, Mr. Avery?"

The solicitor looked a bit sheepish as he drew her away from the open door. He lowered his voice. "The goat is to provide milk for young Wesley, but I didn't have the heart to tell Miss Honoria and Mr. Jamie they couldn't keep their pets if the goat was making the journey."

As if sensing that they were being discussed, the oldest of the Carson children picked up the small furry dog and with large, pleading blue eyes, called, "Our pets will be ever so good, miss. Please don't make us leave them."

Emily suddenly remembered her old pony, Buttercup, whom she had been forced to leave behind so many years before and the pain of that loss on top of losing everything else familiar. She smiled at the boy Mr. Avery had identified as Jamie. "Very well, I suppose we shall have our very own traveling menagerie."

The lad, face beaming, jumped down from the vehicle and moved away as the solicitor stepped forward to assist the other members of the family. It took some minutes for Mr. Avery to pry the birdcage from Honoria's fingers, but at last he convinced her that her birds were indeed going with her. He handed the cage to Emily as he helped the child step to the dusty street.

The birdcage proved heavier than Emily thought, and the parrots squawked and fluttered their wings before settling down. But to Emily's surprise, the large green bird suddenly piped, "Here Kali? Awk! Here Kali?"

"Why, they can speak!" Emily smiled down at Honoria who watched as if the unknown lady meant to make off with the birds.

The little girl with a cherubic face and long, dark ringlets hanging from beneath a ruffled white cap moved a bit closer to her pets. She hooked her small fingers into the woven reed slats of the cage. "Janus talks to Kali. Juno never says a word."

Emily knew that Calcutta had a temple dedicated to the goddess Kali. She smiled at young Honoria's imaginative assumption that the bird had mystical powers. "One of your birds can speak to the Indian goddess?"

Honoria shook her head. "No, to our Kali." The child pointed to the little black ball of fur which squirmed in Jamie's arms as the boy stood some distance away watching the Indian servants unload their trunks. Emily at last understood—one of the parrots had learned to call the dog from hearing the phrase repeated by the children.

Within minutes all the occupants of the carriage, both human and animal, were out of the vehicle. Emily eyed the goat, wondering what they were going to do with such a creature until they boarded the ship. At that moment, Mr. Patel, the hotel owner, arrived with Delia.

It soon became clear to Emily that her inheritance of a fortune was true power. The Hindustani innkeeper stated that if the wealthy Miss Collins wanted to keep a goat, a dog and several birds in her rooms, he had no objections. He suggested, however, that both she and her companions' sensibilities would be better suited— with that the man's nose twitched—if the goat resided in the stable. Emily heartily agreed and allowed the animal to be led away by a hotel employee.

As Mr. Avery and Mr. Patel shepherded the children and the smaller animals into the hotel, Emily looked at Delia with a grin. "It seems that despite your best efforts, I have become the Eccentric Miss Collins after all."

Delia smiled and twined her arm through her friend's as they trailed behind. " 'Tis this unknown Lord Hawksworth who will be saddled with this menagerie, not you, my dear. As long as you can refrain from trying to ride the goat with one of the birds on your head in Hyde Park, I think you can escape that fate."

Emily laughed at the mental picture. Her entry into Society would be delayed until she'd fulfilled her duty to the Carson children by delivering them to Bath. For a moment her thoughts turned to the unknown uncle in England who was about to inherit an entire family, pets included. She could only hope that the gentleman and his wife liked children and animals, for by next spring he would have a surplus of both.

London—1814

A light dusting of snow had fallen the night before, giving the streets of Mayfair a pristine look except where it had been disturbed by early-morning traffic. The large, elegant town coach moved through the icy streets at a sedate pace until the vehicle came to a stop in front of Lord Hawksworth's town house on Park Lane.

A footman in white wig and gold livery climbed down from his rear perch and ambled to the carriage door. It was uncertain if his slow pace was due to the cold or his advanced years, an element he held in common with the coachman. From the vehicle, two ladies of like age descended to the pavement, but the grey of their hair had nothing to do with wigs. Nora, Dowager Countess of Hawksworth, and her companion, Miss Luella Millet, were well advanced into their seventies.

As the ladies shook the wrinkles from their gowns, the footman knocked. Despite the early hour, the butler answered the door in a matter of minutes.

"Ah, Bedows, I see you are as efficient as ever," the dowager remarked as she entered and moved to a fire burning in the elegantly appointed hall.

"You are too kind, my lady." The butler's thin face beneath his white hair showed no pleasure at the compliment. He stoically went about the business of helping the ladies remove their wraps, then ushered them upstairs into the drawing room. "I shall inform his lordship of your arrival."

"You mean warn him, don't you, Bedows?" Lady Hawksworth chuckled. Perhaps it was the light, but she could swear the servant's mouth twitched into a bit of a grin.

"Would your ladyship like refreshments while you wait?"

"That is an excellent suggestion since I have no doubt my grandson will keep us waiting for some time."

The butler made no comment. He closed the door, leaving the ladies alone. Within a very short time he returned with a footman carrying a tray loaded with an assortment of cakes and tea.

The dowager and Miss Millet had already made great inroads into the French cook's efforts and ordered a second pot of tea by the time Lord Hawksworth arrived in the drawing room. His appearance gave no indication of the haste required to get him out of bed and dressed in under an hour.

Oliver Carson, tenth Earl of Hawksworth, was not a dandy, but he took great pride in dressing in the first style of elegance. At present he wore a simply cut dark-green morning coat over a sedate green-striped waistcoat and tan pantaloons. What set him apart from the average man was the elegance of his neckcloth, tied in the Mathematical, a style few could replicate.

As he sauntered into the room to greet his grandmother and her companion, the earl wondered fleetingly what new scandal had reached Lady Hawksworth's ears. It mattered little, for there had been so many over the past years that he'd gotten quite used to being jarred from his bed at some ungodly hour to explain his actions.

He greeted the ladies and had just settled into a chair when his grandmother surprised him from his complacency.

"Do you never read your correspondence?"

Oliver's brows rose slightly. "In truth, Grandmother, I discovered years ago that there is little of interest in the letters people send to me. I rarely pay attention to the post. People who write letters are either asking for something, which is a dead bore, or telling you about something they have done which is an even deadlier bore."

The dowager gave an unladylike grunt at her grandson's jaded attitude. "Well, *I* sent you two letters summoning you to Woburn on a matter of some urgency. Because of your negligence in reading your messages, I have had to make the long drive to London in this wretched weather."

The earl propped his head upon his hand, as if to show how tired he was of explaining himself to his interfering grandmother. "You really should not listen to all the gossip your friends tell you about my wicked deeds, madam. That way you wouldn't have to inconvenience yourself coming to Town to ring a peal over my head."

"But if I told my friends to tell me only your good deeds, my boy, you should never be spoken of again, or so it seems."

Oliver laughed. "Surely I am not as bad as that. Why, only last week I succumbed to Lady Chesterly's entreaties and donated a generous sum to the Foundling Hospital."

Lady Hawksworth gave a snort. "You cannot fool me into believing you gave a thought to some orphaned brats. I have long known your dislike of anyone, and especially children, disrupting your pursuit of pleasure. This Lady Chesterly must be a complete ninny to be taken in by such an obvious ploy."

" 'Twas never her mental prowess or lack thereof that attracted me to the lady, Grandmother." Oliver gave a wicked grin, then turned to the lady's companion. "Do you think I might trouble you for some tea, dear Miss Millet?"

The dowager looked at Miss Millet, who'd been sitting quietly during the exchange, as the spinster blushed at the earl's notice. The ladies exchanged a look which could only be interpreted as "this young man is hopeless." Then the aged companion began to pour a cup of tea for the earl.

Lady Hawksworth was not to be distracted from the true purpose of her visit. "I did not come to discuss your newest paramour, young man. We have far more important matters to discuss. I want to know what you have done about honoring your promise to your late grandfather?"

Oliver took the cup of tea Miss Millet offered him. He bent forward, dropping a lump of sugar into the liquid, using the time to search his memory for a long-forgotten pledge. His grandfather had died some fourteen years earlier. What vow had Oliver foolishly made and forgotten?

At last he looked up at the dowager. "I fear you have me at a disadvantage. I cannot remember having made a promise of any significance to my grandfather."

" 'Tis a sad fact that memory fades as one ages, my boy." The old lady's eyes glittered with amusement.

"I am five-and-thirty, madam, not five-and-sixty. What was this promise?" Oliver snapped, too often amazed at how his grandmother held the ability to prick his pride.

" 'Twas made the night of your twenty-first birthday," the lady announced, watching to see if the date triggered his memory.

The night's events flashed into Oliver's mind for the first time in years. A naive young cawker back then, he'd started the evening with anticipation and delight, thinking himself in love. But Lady Rose had driven a knife into his heart all those years ago. He'd come upon her in the gardens in the arms of Colonel Fenn as she was saying that if Oliver came up to scratch, she would marry him for his title and wealth, but her heart would always belong to the soldier.

The memory was no longer painful, but Oliver remembered he'd spent much of the evening in a haze of misery. He'd only wanted to go away to lick his wounded pride, but instead duty to his family and a good dose of champagne had kept him at the party, pretending to enjoy his night. Had he made some promise to his grandfather during those long hours of self-pity and over-indulgence?

"I cannot remember making a promise to anyone."

Lady Hawksworth's eyes narrowed. "Do not think you shall be able to slip out of your pledge, for I was present when you swore to marry before your thirty-sixth birthday if you had not done your duty before then."

Oliver nearly shattered the fine bone china as his hand tightened on his teacup from shock. Had he foolishly promised the old earl to wed by the end of this year? He *must* have been completely out of his mind. Or at the very least too deep in his cups to know what he was about. He had no desire to become leg-shackled, now or ever.

He set his cup back on the tray and rose, aware of two pair of curious eyes watching him intently. He went to the window and gazed out at the small, well-tended garden, trying to reason his way out of this dilemma.

His thoughts more ordered, he looked back at his grandmother. "If Grandfather requested such a promise, no doubt it was for the sake of a future heir. My brother has provided an heir, and therefore I see no need for me to become entangled in the bonds of matrimony."

Lady Hawksworth rose with surprising agility for one of her years, marching towards her grandson with purpose. The only sound in the room was the rustling of her deep-green skirts. When she stood in front of him, she squared her shoulders as if she were prepared to do battle. "Are you certain you still have an heir? If you ever paid any attention to your correspondence, you would perhaps have noticed there has been no letter from Anna or James for over two years."

"Has it been so long?" Oliver frowned. Had something happened to James and his wife? A sharp pain pierced the earl's chest at the thought that his brother might be dead. He prayed it wasn't true.

"It has, so you must honor your promise to your grandfather. James and his son might have been eaten by tigers or trampled by elephants for all we know."

The earl smiled in spite of the dire possibilities. "I never knew you to have such a lurid imagination, Grandmother."

"Unlike you, I always read Anna's letters. India is a dangerous place. Will you keep your pledge?" The lady watched her grandson with slate-grey eyes.

Oliver suddenly found himself at a standstill. He didn't want a wife. He had females aplenty to amuse him, and when he tired of the whims and demands of one, there was always another to take her place. Females were all alike, after all, more interested in a man's money and rank than in the man himself.

But what did it matter? Didn't most married people of the *ton* go their separate ways? His life would change very little with a marriage of convenience, should he take a proper wife. If something had happened to his brother, it was Oliver's responsibility to produce an heir.

"Very well, Grandmother. I shall honor my promise."

The dowager cocked her head slightly. "Don't think that I will accept one of Hawksworth's Harem as a future granddaughter-in-law. She must be a proper lady without the least taint to her reputation."

Oliver made no comment about his grandparent's use of Society's taunt in referring to all the women who'd been under his protection over the years. Instead he wrapped her arm through his, leading her back to where Miss Millet sat. He was aware that the kind of lady he should marry was one of the very innocent females who bored him to death, but there was nothing for it.

As he settled his grandmother again in her chair, a thought occurred which made him smile. "The difficulty is that I am rarely invited to occasions where delicately bred females are in attendance. I shall have a difficult time finding such a lady."

The dowager's words quickly wiped the smile from Oliver's face. "I have thought of that. Knowing you would do what is proper in honoring your promise to your grandfather, I have approached the Marquess of Halcomb on your behalf. Lady Cora Lane is all that you would want in a wife—beautiful, titled and wealthy, her reputation unimpeachable. The marquess is agreeable to such an arrangement. All you need do is make a morning call to announce your intentions to pay your addresses to the lady and the matter can be quickly settled."

Oliver didn't think he'd had such a black moment since the night he'd discovered Lady Rose's perfidy. Marriage suddenly loomed ominously close. In a moment of desperation, he fabricated a plan and announced, "I shall have to delay my call for the present.

I have engaged a party of friends to go down to Hawks's Lair for several weeks."

"During the height of the Season?" The retiring Miss Millet spoke for the first time since he'd entered the room. Her tone appeared skeptical.

The earl's mind was racing. He would have to invite a party of gentlemen to his home on a moment's notice. Whom could he find to take and how would he entertain them without the possibility of hunting or fishing during the bitterly cold spring? He realized his grandmother was looking at him, her expression as doubtful as her companion's.

"Ladies, my particular friends take little note of the introduction of a bevy of marriage-minded females into Society. I shall call on the marquess when I return next month."

The dowager was quiet for a moment; then she said, "I want you to be content with your wife, Oliver. I think Lady Cora will suit you very well. She won't be one of those foolish creatures who babbles of love and demands her husband dance attendance upon her. She knows what is expected."

Oliver should have been delighted with his grandmother's pronouncement, but somehow it only made his forthcoming marriage appear even less appealing. Still, to reassure the dowager, he said all that was proper about his proposed fiancée.

Some thirty minutes later, the dowager announced that she intended to return to the country that very day. She would await word from her grandson that all the arrangements for his impending marriage were complete.

Oliver halfheartedly encouraged her to stay, but in truth, his mind was intent on searching through his raffish friends for a small group who would be willing to abandon the amusements of the Season and accompany him to Bath. How could he lure a party of men to the countryside? Females, horses and gaming were the entertainments that interested gentlemen most. Oliver decided that, to be safe, he would offer all three diversions to entice his friends out of Town.

After bidding his grandmother and her companion good-bye, he called for his hat, coat and cane. He had a great many arrangements to make. First he would track down his oldest friend, Sir Ethan Russell. The baronet, hopefully, would help him with the arrangement for his impromptu house party. Sir Ethan was well known to the leading actresses of the Season, preferring ladybirds to widows and straying wives. Perhaps he could introduce Oliver to several who might be induced to come and entertain his friends—for a large fee.

No matter what happened, he intended to be in Bath by the end of the week. At the present, all he wanted was to be away from London, from the Marquess of Halcomb's daughter and that ever-looming specter of an impending marriage.

Two

Hawk's Lair Castle, a large Elizabethan structure notable for the ornate domes on the four outer towers, lay some ten miles southwest of Bath at the edge of the Mendip Hills. In the darkness the occupants of the newly arrived vehicle could see little of the looming building except the huge lacquered doors under the arched portico. The brass-studded wood was lit by two oil lanterns fixed into the white stone pediment surrounding the portal.

"We are here at last," Emily announced as her sleeping fellow travelers began to stir beneath the woolen traveling rugs. Hawk's Lair was a welcome sight, since the heated bricks placed in the carriage were now stone cold. She'd had no idea of the trials and tribulations she and Delia would face while journeying the thousands of miles from Calcutta to England with three children and sundry animals. The problems seemed endless— abandonment by the children's nurse at the first port of call, storm-tossed seas followed by becalmed days without a hint of wind, and lastly a bout of illness visited upon the children within days of arriving at Plymouth.

Perhaps the most worrisome of her problems involved the unknown Lord Hawksworth. In the three weeks they'd been stranded at the Hart and Hound in the Devonshire countryside nursing young Wesley and Honoria back to health, she'd sent letters to both his Bath estate and his residence in Town without the least response. Emily was beginning to suspect that she and Delia might end up permanent caretakers of the children. But she knew that would be no hardship, for they'd come to love the trio over the course of their travels together.

The jangle of a team announced the arrival of the cart loaded with their trunks as it drew to a halt behind them. The sound caused the goat, Matilda, to *baa* with misery at having long been cramped on the floor of the coach. Emily reached down and stroked the animal as Jamie summoned Kali from the goat's side. Janus, in his covered cage in the corner, echoed the call.

Swarup opened the door and let down the steps. He tied Matilda's lead rope round her neck and urged her from the vehicle to clear the aisle so the others might step down. Soon everyone, human and animal, was standing on the frozen ground in front of the great oak doors. The Indian handed the goat's leash to Jamie, then went to rap the heavy knocker. As the sound echoed back at them, the giant servant stepped aside for his mistress to speak with whoever answered the summons. The man from Calcutta had not been long in England before he realized that his size and even his dark skin seemed to frighten the average Englishman.

Before the castle door opened, Wesley began to fuss as he squirmed in Delia's arms, wanting only to be in his bed, not understanding why he was awakened so late. Tiny fists rubbed at weary eyes as his whimpers grew louder.

Emily extended her arms and said, "Here, I shall take

him, my dear. You must be exhausted. You have cared for him since we left Wells this afternoon."

Delia surrendered the baby, then took the birdcage from Honoria, who appeared quite exhausted despite wide, curious eyes. Allowing her gaze to rest on her employer, the widow said, "I cannot like the idea of our arriving so late, Emily. You know what the innkeeper at the Hart and Hound said about the earl."

Emily laughed as she patted the baby's back to quiet his cries. "That Lord Hawksworth was a notorious rakehell? Do you fear for our virtue, my dear?"

"Don't be silly. 'Tis only that it might be considered unseemly to be residing at a rake's residence, no matter the reason. I lack sufficient beauty to interest a rake, but you are both lovely and an innocent."

"I doubt his lordship will have the time to give a second glance to two unfashionably dressed females who are about to turn his raffish world upside down."

At that moment a footman opened the door. Dressed in black livery with gold frogging and a neat white wig, he swept the lot with such a look of condescension that Emily wished they'd had the time to be outfitted with new wardrobes.

With a self-assurance she was far from feeling in her drab gray traveling gown and plain poke bonnet, Emily announced, "I should like to see Lord Hawksworth on a private matter."

Speaking with all the arrogance he could muster, the servant, whose name was Martin, intoned, "His lordship is not at home to visitors this evening, madam."

He made as if to shut the door, but to his surprise the female in grey boldly thrust her hand upon the door, stopping him. "Perchance I did not make myself clear. I am here to see his lordship on a matter of some urgency, and these children should not be left standing in the cold."

Martin chewed his lip pensively. He liked the prestige that being employed at the castle netted him at the local tavern. He'd held his position as second footman for nearly a year, but this was the first time he was responsible for handling visitors, Bedows having gone to bed sick early in the evening. As he pondered what he should do about this pushing female, his gaze dropped to the young girl and boy peeking around the woman who was trying to force her way in. At once he was struck with the resemblance the children held with his lordship.

In an instant, the footman guessed that this woman was some soiled dove who'd enjoyed his lordship's favors. Now she was trying to force her way into the castle to dun Lord Hawksworth for blunt for her base-born brats. Straightening with indignation, Martin knew his duty.

"Go about your business, you brass-faced hussy. His lordship don't want your kind darkenin' his doorway. Nor any brats disturbin' his peace. Likely he would call the magistrate to have you thrown in the gaol for immoral behavior and who would blame him." With that the servant stepped forward and extended his arm to give the woman a shove out of the way.

But his hand had barely landed on her shoulder before Martin felt something grip the back of his collar, and his feet flew off the floor. He was jerked about and found himself staring into the black eyes of an insane brown giant with a white sheet wrapped round his head.

"You will not touch my *memsahib* in such a manner! Do you understand?"

Emily watched the footman's mouth open, but words

failed to come out. Swarup gave him another gentle shake and the frightened servant was able to croak, "Yes."

At that moment, the sounds of masculine laughter echoed from the far reaches of the building. Emily, her ire raised by their shabby treatment at the hands of Lord Hawksworth's footman, decided to seek the gentleman without the servant's help. She was beginning to wonder what kind of man Mr. Carson had for a brother, who would allow a servant to turn children away on a bitterly cold night.

"Swarup, put him down. Children, follow me."

The Indian obeyed his mistress. He tossed the footman onto the ground as if he were yesterday's rubbish, causing the fellow's wig to go flying into the gravel. Then Swarup joined the others who filed into the Great Hall of Hawk's Lair.

Emily led the children across the black-and-white marble floor to the oversized fireplace. As they all stood basking in the warmth of the blaze, she surveyed the many white doors that lined the blue walls of the cavernous foyer. Despite her anger, she found herself impressed with the grandeur of Hawk's Lair. The beautiful Elizabethan building might be owned by a rake, but it showed no signs of neglect or impoverishment.

Young Wesley again began to whimper, reminding Emily of her mission. She gently patted his back as her gaze began to rove over the doors closed against the chill of the hall. At last she saw light glowing from under one. She assumed that was where she would find Lord Hawksworth. She marched forward, her little band loyally following her into battle, or so it seemed.

But at that moment, the rapid beat of footsteps sounded and the footman appeared from behind them at a full run. His wig was again perched upon his head, but now the white queue poked out the front like the horn of a rhinoceros. The man planted himself in front of Emily, his hands locked on either side of the door frame in an effort to bar her from entering. Breathless but determined, he announced, "You cannot disturb his lordship."

Emily's amber eyes glittered with a mixture of anger and determination. "Can I not?" She glanced to her servant, and an unspoken message passed between them. Without a word, Swarup's large hand again shot out, grabbing the footman by the collar. The Indian carried his burden back to the middle of the Great Hall, the footman dangling like a marionette, before allowing the subdued Martin's feet back on the ground. As he relinquished his hold, Swarup issued a stern warning for the man to stay away from his *memsahib*.

Emily was seething. She shot Delia a look which did not bode well for the earl, then squared her shoulders and reached for the door handle.

"I say, Hawksworth, where are these dashing chippers you promised? There wasn't even a single housemaid to warm my bed last night," Mr. Malcolm Abbot complained as he peered over his cards at the earl. A pompous man with a vast inherited fortune, he was short and stout, his brown hair going prematurely grey.

The gentlemen had been playing whist since dinner, and Oliver was thoroughly bored with the game and all of his house guests save his old friend, Sir Ethan. The earl, in desperation to find guests, had made the mistake of tossing out the invitation at White's to a lively group of men. Their mood had been jovial as they discussed the delights of Freezeland Lane, the name given to the stretch of the Thames frozen solid for over six weeks and containing a Frost Fair.

Unfortunately, despite the throng's cheerful humor, the only takers to his offer were the portly Mr. Malcolm Abbot, heir to a Northumberland barony, and Mr. Samuel Bonham, a blithe young man called Bones by his friends due to his lean, angular build and his fondness for dicing. Oliver supposed these gentlemen were his punishment for having told his grandmother a falsehood.

If it hadn't been for Sir Ethan, the earl was certain he would have gone insane over the past few days. The burly Scotsman's teasing humor and ready smile helped Oliver keep his sense of humor about this damnable party.

Oliver surveyed his cards with feigned interest before answering the question. "As I mentioned this morning, Miss Colette Devereau and several of the actresses in her company shall arrive at the end of the week. Exactly when depends on the condition of the roads from London." He looked at the clock and wondered how much longer he would have to endure Abbot's inane comments.

Mr. Bonham, his thin blond hair crimped into curls, eyed the card played by Sir Ethan, then, after making a selection to discard, said, "That's a long time to wait for our promised entertainment. With your butler ailing, ain't no saying but that we shall all be out of frame by the time the ladybirds arrive."

Sir Ethan grinned, then in a voice with a soft Scottish lilt said, "Didn't know you were such a devil with the lasses, Bones."

The young man did his best to give a wicked grin,

but looked more the fool than the rogue. "Have to be a devil to steal a march on Hawksworth and his harem."

Oliver stifled a yawn as the play continued. "My reputation is greatly exaggerated, I assure you."

Abbot lowered his cards and made a great show of straightening the ruby ring on his pudgy fingers. "So the tale about you escorting a lightskirt to Lady Willingham's musicale was just a rumor?"

"No, that is true. Avanley wagered me a monkey I couldn't fool the old tartar, but I did." Oliver chuckled at the memory of his next encounter with Lord Willingham after word got about. The fellow had actually crossed the street to avoid him. Oliver might be a rake, but Society knew him for a crack shot.

Bones puckered his brow in thought. "And the story about having to climb out a second-story window and down a trellis when Lady Shotwell's husband arrived home unexpectedly?"

"Well, that is true as well. But that was years ago." Oliver frowned, amazed at how many of his exploits were common knowledge.

Sir Ethan snorted. He'd been friends with Oliver for over ten years and knew the worse firsthand. "As you can see, Lord Hawksworth's reputation is all exaggerated. Clearly he is a much maligned choir boy."

The gentlemen laughed.

The game then resumed. Oliver informed the group that his groom had discovered there was to be a mill at Marksbury the following afternoon and proposed they go. He named the combatants. The weather would be the determining factor, since the bitter cold and snows of winter had been as relentless throughout March as in February. The company was in agreement that a bout of fisticuffs would be an excellent diversion.

The card players grew quiet when the sounds of voices could be heard coming from the hall. All looked expectantly at the door, thinking the female entertainment had arrived early. But to Oliver's utter amazement, his drawing room door was thrust open without so much as a knock and a pair of drably gowned females, three children and several animals marched into the drawing room as if it were their own.

Curious as well as angered by the interruption, the earl's gaze swept the women as he and the others politely rose. His first thought was that Martin had better be dead because if he wasn't, Oliver was likely to kill him for allowing this shocking collection into his drawing room.

His gaze quickly riveted on the female who carried a baby. He could tell little about her features, which were obscured by a drab poke bonnet, but her plain garb, which encased a shapely feminine figure, looked much like that of a governess or vicar's wife. Unlike the others, who hovered hesitantly at the door, she made straight for the table.

With surprising agility for a female of her size, she lifted the baby up and sat him right in the middle of the green baize table atop the whist deck. She appeared heedless of the banknotes scattered about, as if money were of no importance in the scheme of things. She rounded on the earl with little hesitation. "Lord Hawksworth, despite your servant's efforts to bar me from this house, I am here to deliver your family to you."

Oliver's stunned gaze scanned the children at the door, then dropped to the child sitting in front of him. The baby, too young to understand the drama of the situation, picked up a brightly colored card to inspect, then began to chew on the edge while gazing up with bright blue eyes. Why, the child was his very image! But Oliver was certain he didn't know this woman, nor had he ever fathered any children, to his knowledge.

At last finding his tongue, the earl barked, "Madam, what is the meaning of this intrusion?"

Before the lady could speak, Abbot rudely interrupted, "I say, Hawksworth, 'tis plain as the nose on your face. Your lady has come for blunt to feed this litter. Isn't Bonham who is the devil here."

Oliver frowned at the man beside him. "Sir, if you like the present size and shape of the nose on *your* face, you will kindly refrain from interfering in this matter."

Malcolm Abbot's face turned deadly white and he took a step back. But Bones chuckled, even as he peered at the visitor through his quizzing glass. "Not your usual style, old man. More a peahen than a bird of paradise."

Oliver fell silent, glaring at the woman who stared defiantly back. What else could his guests think when this woman arrived with a trio of brats bearing a remarkable resemblance to him? The whole situation left him speechless.

In the lengthening silence the woman spoke in a voice full of challenge. "Well, sir, what have you to say?"

Sir Ethan cleared his throat. A tall man with an athletic build, he got behind the earl's guests and nudged each in the back. "Gentlemen, I think it time we took our leave while our host discusses this private matter with the lady."

Mr. Abbot and Mr. Bonham, despite their curiosity, knew the better part of valor was retreat where Hawksworth was concerned. Each quickly said good night and departed for their rooms. But Sir Ethan, while moving to the door, remained in the hope that he might help his friend in some way.

At last Oliver gathered his thoughts and spoke his mind. "Madam, I don't know who you are or what your game is. I don't care. But if you take these untidy brats and leave, I shall not find it necessary to call a constable for this prank."

"Prank, sir? I did not travel thousands of miles to play a jest on the most odious man it has ever been my misfortune to meet. I am Miss Emily Collins, and these children you malign are your niece and nephews, which in my opinion is an unfortunate circumstance for them. You, Lord Hawksworth, are now their guardian."

Oliver's bleak gaze shifted back to the baby on the table, who was now happily mangling every last playing card within his reach. In a choked whisper, the earl asked, "And my brother and his wife are . . . ?" He could not bring himself to think of James being dead despite their bitter quarrel and not having seen him in over ten years.

Emily watched the pain and realization settle into the gentleman's blue eyes. Even as she experienced rage at this arrogant man, she felt a sudden rush of sympathy. Her voice softened as she gave him the news. "I fear Mrs. James Carson passed away giving birth last year. Of your brother's fate, I cannot tell you, but he was gravely ill when his solicitor requested that I bring the children to you. I am certain Mr. Avery, your brother's man of business, will write when there is news."

The earl bowed his head and walked to the fireplace. He stood in his grief with his back to his visitors. No one spoke a word, giving his lordship a moment to fathom the dark news.

But the silence of the room was pierced when Matilda, always looking for food, decided the yellow tablecloth beside her might be tasty and pulled it off the small occasional table, sending a shower of family miniatures to the Oriental rug.

There was a sudden bustle of children and adults trying to recover the pictures from the floor and to right the cloth. Kali barked at the disturbance and the parrots joined in the chorus by squawking beneath their cover. Matilda, frightened by the commotion, dashed to the other side of the room, taking refuge behind a painted screen.

Delia, having no reason to converse with his lordship, hurried to retrieve the troublesome animal and led him out into the hall. Sir Ethan followed the lady, leaving only Emily and the children to finish the task of righting things.

Emily, having just set the last miniature back into place, realized that his lordship was again standing at the table watching his youngest nephew with distaste as the child shredded the pasteboard deck. All traces of mourning were gone from his handsome face.

When his gaze settled on her, Emily had to stifle a gasp. He was a handsome man with raven-black hair framing a rugged, well-defined face. But a chill raced down her spine at his cold stare.

"Miss Collins, I fully intend to honor my obligation to my brother. I want you to understand, however, that I shall not tolerate these children disrupting my household. You are expected to keep them quiet and in the nursery when I am in residence. I demand that you behave in a more decorous manner than you have this evening if you wish to keep your position. I—"

"My lord, I would not work for you if I were penniless." By now Emily's temper had got the better of her. Hands on her hips, she continued, "I am not the children's governess nor is Mrs. Keaton, my companion. We simply brought the children as an act of kindness, something I would guess *you* know little about."

A muscle twitched in the earl's angular jaw, but he made no retort. Instead he asked, "Then where is their nurse?"

"Why, the last time I saw her she was disappearing down a street in Madras." Emily smiled benignly.

"Are you telling me you have no female servant whatsoever to attend these children?"

Emily wasn't certain what the expression on the earl's face indicated, but she could swear it was one of near fear. She and Delia had discussed hiring someone, but thought it best to leave the matter to the children's guardian. "My companion and I have seen to the children's needs. But I should think one of your housemaids can take charge until you can bestir yourself to employ a nurse and governess."

"But I have no housemaids or females of any kind in residence in the castle." The earl stared at his nephew as if the child had grown a second head.

"No female of any kind?" That gave Emily pause. Then her eyes narrowed. "I must suppose no respectable person in the county would allow his daughter to work for an infamous rake."

His lordship's head turned sharply as he looked down his nose at her. "I have never forced my attentions on a female in my employ, madam, even in my salad days."

Emily hesitated a moment before making a comment, her mind busy trying to decide what must be done. There was no doubt that she would stay and help until the children were settled, but she saw no reason to let

Lord Hawksworth know that. The indifferent lord needed to be taught a lesson.

"It is unfortunate you employ no maids, but that is not my concern." She went to the table and had to stifle a laugh as she gave Wesley a kiss. The child was now covered in tiny red and white flecks of the remnants of the shredded whist deck. Then she walked back to where Honoria and Jamie forlornly waited, giving each a kiss.

"Be good for your uncle. I shall write to inquire how you like your new home. Good-bye."

Without a backward glance, Miss Collins walked out the door and closed it behind her. Oliver was appalled to be left alone with his young relations. He knew nothing about caring for children. He eyed the boy and girl with anxiety, then turned his gaze on the unkempt baby crawling about on the table beside him. The tot was in his own world, babbling and tossing the few remaining undamaged cards to the floor.

Without the least warning, the little girl burst into heart-wrenching sobs, and her brother stared at his uncle as if he'd lost his best friend. The tiny black creature, which Oliver had decided was a dog despite his miniature size, began to bark at him with zeal. What was he to do with this lot? He hadn't the least notion.

He really couldn't think due to the din. All he was certain of was that he couldn't manage this troublesome lot without a female, and at the moment the only females around were the annoying Miss Collins and her companion. Then he realized that perhaps if he were contrite enough, he could convince the termagant not to leave just yet, at least until he'd hired a new nurse.

"Do be quiet, girl," Oliver barked. Honoria sputtered to a hiccuping silence. About to follow Miss Collins, the earl suddenly realized he couldn't leave his nephew on the table unattended. He scooped the baby up under his arm like a sack of potatoes, a shower of card bits falling to the floor, and made toward the door. But the small ball of black fur with legs reached the portal first, growling and barking at him as well as blocking his path.

"You, boy, get this hairy rat out of my way."

The lad obediently whistled, and the small creature ran to him. Oliver ordered the older children to come with him, then he tore the door open and hurried into the hall. To his relief he discovered the ladies in conversation with Sir Ethan.

He marched straight up to the trio, the baby wiggling under his arm and babbling incoherently. "Miss Collins, I must have a word with you." He did his best to look contrite, even though he wanted to order her to remember he was an earl and therefore someone to be treated with respect. Her cold glare gave him pause. He was quite unused to females taking him in dislike.

There was not the least bit of remorse reflected in her amber eyes for abandoning him with these children, but he was surprised to see she'd removed her bonnet as if she meant to stay. It gave him his first unobstructed view of her. Light brown curls were pulled into an unflattering knot at her neck. Her face was delicately carved, but her manner was haughty. He couldn't decide if he thought her attractive or not, since the only feature he could admire as she watched him were her fine amber eyes.

Remembering his mission to appease her, he cleared his throat. He had a thousand things he would like to say about her conduct, but instead he forced himself to say, "Pray, allow me to apologize for the reception you have received here tonight. This has all been a simple misunderstanding, I assure you." He could see that his words were having little effect as she stared back at him. Desperate, he pleaded, "You cannot leave me here without some assistance. The children trust you and Mrs. Keaton. Surely they would be far happier not to be abandoned to strangers who haven't the least notion of how to meet their needs."

Emily cast her gaze downward, not wanting his lordship to see the satisfaction glowing there. So the arrogant lord was admitting he needed help. He'd made it clear in the drawing room he would be an absentee guardian who would leave the children to be raised by paid servants, not wanting his life disrupted. Not something she would want for Jamie, Honoria and Wesley— or any child for that matter. She was convinced that if he came to know his young wards, he couldn't resist them.

At last she raised her chin, staring into those mesmerizing blue eyes. "Mrs. Keaton and I shall stay and help the children settle in, for their sakes. You will require a nurse for Wesley and a governess with proficiency in Latin and History to prepare Jamie for Eton as well as to instruct Honoria."

Forgetting all his good intentions and without a thought to the consequences, Oliver barked, "Madam, I don't need you to tell me what must be done. I know what is needed for my wards." Then, seeing Miss Collins's back stiffen, he remembered he was trying to appease the lady. He could ill afford to alienate this difficult female, at least for tonight. It took great effort, but at last he was able to modulate his tone to the proper degree. "Please, forgive my temper. I can only say the shock of your sudden arrival has made me forget my manners."

The lady gave a nod of her head, then extended her arms to Lord Hawksworth. A look of surprise crossed his face—as if he'd want to embrace such a contrary creature—until he realized that she wanted to take possession of his squirming nephew. He righted young Wesley, sending a new shower of card bits to the marble floor, and handed him to her.

She turned to her own servant, who stood quietly against the wall holding Matilda's rope. "Swarup, show his lordship's man what is to be unloaded."

Lord Hawksworth's eyes widened at the sight of the large Indian, but he made no comment. Instead, he ordered Martin to summon assistance, remove the animals and to see to Miss Collins's and Mrs. Keaton's comfort. Then he announced that he and Sir Ethan would be in the library if needed. With that the gentlemen bowed as the ladies were led upstairs.

At the landing, Emily glanced back. The earl was wiping his coat as if he could rid himself not only of the bits of colored pasteboard, but his responsibility as well. No doubt his plan was to ignore his niece and nephews as much as possible, but that was not in the children's best interest. A rake might be an unlikely father, but it didn't mean he couldn't be shown how to be a loving one, and Emily promised herself that was just what she intended to do before she left Hawk's Lair.

Three

Lord Hawksworth and Sir Ethan made a hasty retreat to the library when the hulking brown servant began to order the castle's footmen to stack a collection of trunks and woven baskets in the Great Hall. After closing the door, the earl went straight to his desk and poured a large measure of brandy from the cut-crystal decanter into two glasses.

Sir Ethan, taking a seat in front of the fire, accepted the drink, then waited for his lordship to be seated before he spoke. "I'm dreadfully sorry about your brother and his wife. Were you close?"

Oliver slumped back in the leather armchair, swirling the honey-brown liquid in the glass. "At one time." He fell silent and gazed into the fire, lost in memories of long ago when he and James had been best friends. At last remembering his manners, he looked at his friend. "I tried to talk him out of going to the Indies, but he wouldn't listen."

The baronet nodded. "Determined to make his own fortune?"

The earl took a sip of his brandy. "Our dear departed stepmother had convinced him that I was denying him his rightful share of our father's estate. He threw the offer of an estate in Yorkshire and fifteen-thousand pounds per annum back in my face. Said he would go to Calcutta and come back a nabob, to prove he didn't need my meager castoffs."

Sir Ethan's brows rose. The offer was far more generous than most younger sons would ever receive. "To be sure, every man must follow his own path. He was very young at the time he and his lady departed. My guess would be that he regretted his words many times over the past ten years."

With a sigh, Oliver ran a hand through his hair, mussing the neat arrangement. "I suppose you are correct."

"Really, old fellow, you must look on the bright side of all this. You will be able to raise your heir and the so-called spare without the inconvenience of a wife."

Hawksworth cast his friend a knowing glance. He was well aware that Sir Ethan had been briefly married nearly fifteen years ago. He never spoke of his late wife, but there had been rumors of an unhappy union. The ladies of Society often lamented that the baronet, a handsome man with his auburn hair and muscular build, never formed a permanent relationship after his period of mourning. It was clear that the man thought of a wife as an encumbrance.

" 'Tis certain I know of one lady who would make a very inconvenient wife." Oliver raised his gaze towards the ceiling to indicate Miss Collins.

The baronet chuckled. "But a dashedly good mother, if her hearty defense of your niece and nephews is any indication. Reminded me of my own dear mother in that manner."

The earl made no comment. He had few memories of his own mother and very bitter ones of his stepmother. Childless herself, Lady Agatha had done her best to pit the brothers against each other from the day she married their father.

Just then a knock sounded on the door, and Martin entered the room. He came to stand facing his lordship to give his report, but he fell silent, seeming to hesitate as the earl gazed at him expectantly.

Oliver, sensing some difficulty, asked, "Have the ladies and my young charges all been comfortably settled?"

"They have, my lord. But Miss Collins said the nursery is a bit of a disgrace. Ordered us to put Master Jamie and Miss Honoria in the rooms across from her. I had Sam bring down a cradle and the little one is in with Mrs. Keaton."

Oliver arched a single brow and grinned at his friend. So Miss Collins was being difficult again. Looking back at the footman, the earl inquired, "And the menagerie? What did you do with the animals?"

"Sent the goat to the stables, the birds are in Miss Honoria's room and that little black furry creature is in with the young master."

"Despite looking like a hairy rodent, I do assure you it is a dog, for I have never heard of barking rats, even in the East Indies. You have done well, Martin. That will be all."

The footman lingered. "My lord, there is the matter of that great heathen brute Miss Collins brought."

"Put him in a room near the other servants." Oliver didn't understand the problem. There had to be any number of rooms vacant in the servants' quarters since he kept a minimum staff at the castle due to his rare visits.

"But . . . well, my lord, the lads is scared to have him on the same floor."

It had been a long, trying day. Oliver was losing his patience. "Why? He is a servant like any other, despite his brown skin and turban."

Martin paled visibly at his master's tone, but stood his ground. "When Colonel Pettigrew was here last year, he and his man had just returned from the Indies. The batman told us that men out there carry great poisonous snakes around in baskets and charm them out to do wicked deeds. This Swap chap has several such baskets with him."

Oliver heard Sir Ethan laugh under his breath. Having had quite enough of his peace disturbed for one night, the earl snapped, "I believe Miss Collins called him Swarup, and the baskets are no doubt filled with clothes or that goat would have been halfway to London in fright by now. But to ease your mind, put the Indian on the maids' floor, since it is empty, and tell the lads to lock their doors. No snake, charmed or otherwise, can get through a locked barrier."

Martin seemed to relax at his lordship's pronouncement. "Very good, my lord." With a purposeful step he exited the room.

"What else is going to disrupt us this evening?"

Sir Ethan grinned. "You have become too used to the ordered routine of your life, Oliver. I think perhaps instantaneous fatherhood might be the making of you."

"Or the death of me."

Both men chuckled. Then Oliver settled back and again sipped at his brandy. A questioning expression came to his face. "How the deuce does one charm a dangerous snake?"

"I believe the colonel spoke on the subject one night when we were blowing a cloud together. He said that in Calcutta they believe that when the viper is charmed by the playing of a flute, he will not bite."

Mention of the exotic land made the earl wonder what Miss Collins had been doing there. No doubt she had been employed as someone's governess and was turned off for her insolence. As his thoughts centered on the woman who'd brought chaos to his life, he suspected tonight's contretemps about the children would not be their last. She certainly was like no other woman of his acquaintance. Why, when he was at his most charming, she'd been little affected. "I could wish that such a flute would work on females as well."

"Are you thinking of the resolute Miss Collins? I suspect her bark is much worse than her bite." Sir Ethan put his empty glass on the table beside his chair and rose.

"That is easy for you to say. 'Twas not your hide she was flaying with her sharp tongue." The earl tossed off the last of his brandy and joined his friend. They headed for the door.

"Don't tell me that you, who are famous for handling women, are going to allow a slip of a girl who speaks her mind to run roughshod over you."

"Absolutely." Oliver laughed at his friend's expression as he opened the door. "That is, until I hire a nurse and a governess to take charge of my young relatives. Then our outspoken Miss Collins had better watch her step."

The gentlemen exited the library and made their way up to their rooms for the night. Sir Ethan wondered if it wasn't Oliver Carson who might lose the battle of wills with his unexpected house guest. If he was any judge of character, he thought life in India could not have been easy for Miss Collins. After all, it was a man's world there, more so than even in England.

There could be little doubt that there was a great strength of character to a woman who'd managed to get herself, a companion, three children and sundry animals all the way to England with the help of only a single servant. She was not some simpering Society miss, pampered and idle, but a woman who knew her own mind. In truth, she might be more than even his lordship could handle.

As the gentlemen said their good nights, the baronet decided this impromptu house party might prove far more entertaining than he'd ever imagined. Not merely because of Oliver's circumstances, but Sir Ethan might amuse himself with the children's two delightful companions.

While the gentlemen were finding their way to their beds in the east wing, the ladies were ensconced in elegant chambers in the west wing. With the children now fast asleep after glasses of warm milk, Emily and Delia had come together on the pretext of having some refreshments, but each was eager to know what the other thought of Lord Hawksworth.

"Put the tray here," Emily directed the servant, as Delia sat beside the fire in the small, elegant sitting room between their bedchambers. The apartment had a feminine quality, with pale pink curtains and pink-and-white striped satin chairs and pink damask sofas.

Martin put down the silver tray holding the tea and cinnamon toast Miss Collins had requested, then bowed. "Will that be all, miss?"

Emily looked to see if Delia required anything further.

When her companion gave her a negative nod, Emily smiled at the footman. "I believe we are quite settled for the night. Don't wait up for us to finish. I shall bring the tray to the kitchen in the morning when I come for the children's breakfast."

Martin's brown eyes widened. "You mustn't do that, miss. Never set foot in Antoine's kitchen. 'Tis a rule of the castle that no female may enter."

"No doubt so ordered by his lordship." Really, Emily thought, the arrogant man was not to be tolerated.

"That Frenchie cook don't cotton to females interferin' with his work, miss. His lordship says that the fellow is such a wonder with them sauces, that if he don't want women about, there will be no women in the castle." Martin shook his head in puzzlement that the earl would allow his cook such power. The footman missed having a tickle in the stillroom with one of the scullery maids now and again, but that had all ceased when Antoine arrived in the earl's employ nearly a year ago.

Emily felt her cheeks warm. She had wrongly accused the earl of being unable to control his baser needs as the reason for the lack of maids at the castle. She dismissed her error as a reasonable assumption anyone might have made about a notorious rake. Still, how absurd to allow a mere servant to control one's entire household!

A soft cough from Delia brought Emily out of her musing. She realized that Martin was waiting to be dismissed. "Then if I cannot go to the kitchens, I shall leave the tray here for you to take down in the morning. Pray wait on me at eight on the morrow, and I shall give instructions on what the children will require from this tyrant of the board."

With that the footman bowed. "Very good, Miss Collins."

As the door closed behind the departing servant, Emily took her seat at the table and began to pour out the tea. The pair, being quite famished, ate for several moments before Delia interrupted the silence.

"He is very handsome."

Emily knew at once to whom her friend was referring, but chose to deliberately misunderstand. "I especially liked Sir Ethan's auburn hair and the slight Scottish burr."

"You know I did not mean the baronet, though he is handsome in his own way." Delia stared down into her teacup for a moment, then settled her penetrating gaze on her mistress and friend. "You always had your uncle's protection at the few assemblies we attended in Calcutta. Things are quite different here. I suggest that you reestablish communication with your family. You must surely have some male relation who would provide protection from fortune hunters, my dear. You must exercise caution. Particularly with a gentleman like the earl, who appears to be a notorious rake."

Emily took the last bite of toast and chewed for several minutes. At last brushing the crumbs from her fingers, she vowed, "Oh, there are any number of Collins men who will spring from the woodwork once it is known I am in Town, but I want none of them lingering about. As for Lord Hawksworth, there is no need for him to know any of my circumstances while I am at Hawk's Lair. Once I am certain he is prepared to be a proper guardian, we shall depart for London." Emily had learned the lesson early that a fortune or lack thereof mattered a great deal to many people.

"Just how do you plan to make his lordship behave

kindly to his wards, my dear? He has a house full of guests and will likely pay little heed to you, me or the children over the course of the next few days."

Emily's mouth tilted slyly, which gave Delia pause. In truth it was more of a mischievous grin than a smile. Clearly Lord Hawksworth's peaceful house party was about to be disturbed.

"I have been giving the matter due thought. I believe I have a way to eliminate all the distractions at the castle, but I shall not tell you my plan for I have not worked out all the details." Seeing Delia about to protest, Emily added, "Not another word about his lordship or the children. It is quite late and there is much to do in the morning, so I shall bid you good night."

Mrs. Keaton rose with reluctance, but the look on her lovely face revealed that she was filled with worry about her mistress's mysterious plan.

Emily came round the table and gave her a hug. "Don't worry. I shall do nothing outrageous. Just a bit of dissembling to achieve my goal. After all, we want the best life for the children and I mean to see they have that."

Delia nodded, then wished Emily good night. She had never known her employer to do anything scandalous, so she would trust in her once again for the children's sake. Still, she thought it best that the head of the Collins family should be informed that Emily might be in some danger at Hawk's Lair, especially if the earl thought her a penniless female. With that thought in mind, Delia determined to send a letter that very night to Squire Joshua Collins in Coventry to inform him of his niece's return to England and her current location.

Unaware of Delia's great concern for her mistress's reputation and confident in her own ability to handle

the earl, Emily entered her own room. She eyed her
trunks sitting beside the wardrobe and uttered a mild
curse regarding the unknown Antoine who'd barred
maids from the household. She would have to unpack
her clothes herself.

A variety of colorful India muslins greeted her as she
opened the lid. The gowns weren't the height of fashion,
dating to last year, before her uncle died, but they would
have to do until she reached London. She wanted to
look her best when she went down to breakfast in the
morning, and one could not do that in a badly crushed
gown.

Choosing a blue-and-white checked gown with a
matching indigo-blue velvet spenser trimmed with white
lace on the long sleeves and round the neck, she hung
it over a straight-backed chair, which she positioned in
front of the fire. Then she donned her nightrail and
climbed into bed, all the while planning what she would
say to the gentleman at breakfast.

As she was about to drift into sleep, the face of Lord
Hawksworth flashed in her mind. Delia was correct; he
was very handsome. But Emily vowed not to allow that
to affect her in any way. The children were what was
important. With that thought, she drifted to sleep.

A spring thaw finally came to Somersetshire the following morning, as the sun rose to melt the snow and
ice. Lord Hawksworth rose early, deciding to go immediately to Bath to hire a nurse and governess for his
wards. The warming weather would allow him to travel
in his phaeton, but he knew the roads would quickly
thaw to muddy bogs if he lingered too long at his business.

During a hasty breakfast, the earl informed his butler, still suffering the effects of a cold but determined to fulfill his duties, of the additions to his household. Bedows expressed his sympathies, then informed his lordship of the agency where he would most likely be able to quickly employ a respectable servant and governess.

Oliver requested that the butler inform the gentlemen that the visit to the mill in Marksbury would go on as planned. The earl had every intention of being back at Hawk's Lair before noon. About to don his driving gloves, he remembered the ladies and children.

"Bedows, inform Miss Collins that my niece and nephews are not to be allowed out of the nursery today. I do not wish my guests disturbed."

The butler's grey brows jerked upward but a moment, then settled back to their proper position. "Begging your pardon, my lord, but are you certain that is what you wish me to say? I don't know this lady, but nothing makes one more contrary than to be ordered not to do something. May I suggest that it might be better to *request* that the ladies not take the children outside, due to the danger of the melting snow and ice? I could suggest that they might like to inspect the trunks of toys and books in the attic."

Oliver stared at the old man a moment. He'd never known the butler to question an order before. But then, Martin might have informed the fellow about Miss Collins's unconventional conduct the night before. Bedows was correct. The lady wouldn't likely remain in the nursery all day, especially if Oliver ordered it. "Very well, Bedows. Do what will best contain the ladies and my wards to the upper floors."

With that, the earl departed, confident that his able butler would make certain that his guests were not disturbed. But he had not reckoned with Miss Collins's determination.

Some two hours after his lordship had set out for Bath, the other guests began to trickle down to the breakfast parlor. Mr. Abbot and Bones were full of questions about the mysterious females and children when Sir Ethan arrived to break his fast. But the baronet had never suffered from a loose tongue, and so he informed the curious gentlemen that his lordship would tell them as much or as little of his personal affairs as he wished.

Sir Ethan guided the gentlemen to the safer discussion of the opponents in the afternoon's coming mill. Wagers were being placed on the opposing bruisers when the door to the breakfast room opened and Miss Emily Collins stepped in, pausing for effect.

The gentlemen rose, staring at the vision before them. Gone was the drab mouse in the gray traveling gown. In her place stood a lovely young woman. The severe bun had been replaced with a knot of soft brown curls through which a blue ribbon was entwined. The lady wore an elegant morning gown which complemented her figure and made Bones lift his quizzing glass the better to admire her.

"Good morning, gentlemen."

The baronet came round the table. "Miss Collins, you are looking bonny this fine morn." Taking her hand, he led her to the table where the others waited, curiosity glinting in their faces. The Scotsman quickly made the introductions, with no explanation as to who or what the lady was to his lordship. The two gentlemen were full of grandiose compliments, which only made the lady laugh.

"Pray, be seated, gentlemen. Your meals grow cold

and I do not intend to dine, but came to speak with Lord Hawksworth on an urgent matter."

Mr. Abbot and Mr. Bonham returned to their breakfast but with less interest than usual. Sir Ethan remained at the lady's side. "I fear you will not find his lordship here, Miss Collins. Bedows tells me he went to Bath this morning, but is expected to return soon. Is there anything I can do to aid you?"

Emily bit her lip pensively. Her plan had involved the earl, but with his lordship gone, she realized it might prove easier to accomplish without him. She glanced at the gentlemen who stared at her with avid interest. Taking a breath, she launched into her speech. "I fear one of the children appears to be coming down with the measles."

Malcolm Abbot's fork clattered to his plate. His round face grew red and he babbled, "Measles! I have never had the malady. I cannot like this turn of events. What does Hawksworth mean by bringing a collection of disease-ridden brats into his home?"

The others stared at the frantic gentleman, but they had no notion he had suffered from a morbid fear of illness much of his life, having lost two younger brothers to an inflammation of the lungs and fever years earlier. Abruptly, he rose and without speaking to anyone in particular, announced, "I have just remembered an important engagement in Town. Sir Ethan, you must give Hawksworth my regrets, but I must depart immediately."

Mr. Bonham rose with less urgency, but there was a hint of uncertainty in his gaunt features. " 'Tis but a childhood complaint, but ain't something I would relish coming down with. Give my compliments to the earl and say I've gone with Abbot."

With that, the gentlemen exited the breakfast parlor without finishing their meals, making a wide arc around the bearer of the ill tidings as if she were a carrier of the affliction herself. Emily was so delighted with the success of her plan that she quite forgot herself and a smile tipped her lips as the door closed.

Sir Ethan, gazing at the lady as he mentally lamented the illness of the wee bairn, was stuck with the notion that Miss Collins seemed a bit cheery for one who was about to nurse a sick child. When the lady became aware of his scrutiny, her expression sobered.

"Sir, do not let me detain you. I shall fully understand if you wish to flee the children's sickness."

All at once the baronet understood that secret smile. Miss Collins had come to rid the house of his lordship's guests. Not that he could blame her. If he had any offspring, he was certain he wouldn't want a pair of loose fish like Abbot and Bonham hanging about. Clearly she wanted him gone as well, but Sir Ethan knew he couldn't miss seeing Oliver's face when he learned that the lady had cleared the house during his lordship's absence. The Scotsman couldn't resist grinning at her as he announced, "Well, I dislike disappointing such a bonny lass, but I had the measles years ago in Scotland."

Emily was only mildly dissatisfied that her ruse had not removed all of his lordship's guests. Sir Ethan's behavior had been all that was proper last night, and he perhaps might give Lord Hawksworth good advice about being a responsible guardian, as he appeared some years more mature than the earl. "Oh, I am pleased to hear you are not in any danger of falling ill. But you must excuse me, sir. I cannot leave dear Delia to manage all three of the children alone."

Sir Ethan watched the door close behind Miss Collins. With a chuckle, he sat down to finish his breakfast and await the return of his friend.

"So the pretty blond lass is Delia." His thoughts shifted from the earl and his lovely tormentor to the lady he'd spoken with the night before. She was not like her friend, with her gentle reserved ways. Nor was she like the bored, sophisticated females that crowded the *ton*. She was like a warm breeze come to thaw his frozen heart.

The baronet gave a shout of laughter at his sudden poetic turn. Tossing his napkin to the table, he rose and decided to walk to the village to take care of a small matter before the earl returned.

Lord Hawksworth entered the castle some thirty minutes after the coach carrying Mr. Abbot and Mr. Bonham had departed for Town. Unaware of the defection of most of his guests, Oliver went straight to his library to summon Bedows.

He informed the butler that a Mrs. Milly Waters would be arriving that evening and she was to take over the duties of nurse to the children. He hadn't been so fortunate in his search for a governess. He'd been disappointed to learn that the agency would have to advertise for a governess who taught Latin, not having one at present.

He hoped that the newly hired nurse would be sufficient for the troublesome Miss Collins. If he were lucky, she and her female companion might be on their way in the morning, leaving him and his friends to their planned amusements. But in truth, he knew that he and James owed the ladies a great debt for returning the children to England, and manners demanded that they be allowed to remain as long as they wished to recover from the arduous journey.

When Bedows turned to leave, Oliver halted him. "Where are the gentlemen?"

The butler cleared his throat. "My lord, Mr. Abbot and Mr. Bonham—" Just then a knock sounded on the library door, and it opened to reveal Sir Ethan.

"So you are back, Hawksworth. Was your mission a success?"

Oliver dismissed Bedows, but was puzzled by the look of what appeared to be relief on the old man's face. Perhaps the man was still out of curl with his cold.

As the baronet strolled in, the earl's attention was diverted by the sight of a package in his friend's hand, but Hawksworth asked no prying questions. Instead he directed the gentleman to the fireplace, where he joined him. "Not entirely. I was able to engage a nurse, but I fear Miss Collins's requirements for a governess were such that I shall have to wait to find a lady with the knowledge to teach Latin."

Sir Ethan laid the small bound bundle on the table. "Never hired a governess myself, but one would want the best for one's heir. Do you think there *is* a female that reads Latin?"

The earl gave a slight shrug as he stretched his long legs out towards the fire, crossing them at the ankle. "I cannot say, but we shall soon find out. 'Tis unfortunate that the local living is currently vacant so I cannot enlist the vicar to instruct the boy. Where are Abbot and Bones? We must leave soon if we are to reach Marksbury and find a good vantage point to view the mill."

A grin tipped Sir Ethan's mouth. "So, Bedows didn't tell you the news."

With a sinking feeling, Oliver shook his head. He didn't know why, but he was certain that whatever this news was, Miss Collins was going to be involved. She'd scarcely been in his life for twelve hours and already things were in a turmoil. "What has transpired?"

"It seems one of the children has come down with the measles—or so our lovely lady newly arrived from the Indies announced at breakfast."

Oliver watched his friend grin and waggle his auburn brows. "You seem doubtful."

The baronet nodded. "Aye, there was a look about the lass this morning that wasn't quite right. Almost gleeful as the gentlemen announced their departure. Seemed anxious for me to join them in their mad dash back to London."

Oliver shifted his gaze to the flames. Was one of his young wards truly sick, or was Miss Collins playing some deep game? After all, he knew nothing about this female, nor had his brother for that matter. The solicitor's letter informed him that the lady had been chosen merely because she was the first Englishwoman leaving Calcutta. Was she an adventuress planning to use his young relatives to prolong her stay at the castle?

The image of the lady's face came to him, and he remembered her cutting remarks and glittering, angry eyes. If she were planning something of that nature she would have been far more accommodating instead of raging at him so strongly. Still, she seemed to be insinuating herself into his wards' affairs. He didn't know what she was up to, but he would find out.

He went to the bell rope, about to summon the vexatious lady to the library, then decided he would go to her. Perhaps catch her out in whatever little plot she had schemed.

"I think I shall pay a visit to the nursery and see which, if any, of the children are ill."

Sir Ethan rose, picking up his package. "Before you go, I have something which might help you."

Oliver took the small bundle wrapped in brown paper. He looked at his friend, who nodded his head to indicate that he should open the gift. He untied the string and the paper fell away.

Sir Ethan arched one brow. "If all else fails, try this to charm the lady."

The earl fingered the small wooden musical instrument. "I think it would take a flute the size of a cannon to enchant the staunch Miss Collins." With that he tucked the small flute into his pocket and marched out of the room. He went up the stairs to the third floor. With each step his indignation and anger at the lady who'd disrupted his house party grew.

The sight of Swarup standing in front of the nursery door jarred the earl a bit from his certainty that Miss Collins was playing some nefarious game. Did penniless young females have personal servants? And who was Mrs. Keaton in this drama? As he neared the door where the manservant stood, the chant of a nursery rhyme could be heard coming from behind the portal.

Without hesitation Swarup bowed, then opened the door for the earl, who stepped into the room just in time to see Miss Collins, Honoria and Jamie all fall down as the rhyme had ordered. There was a great deal of laughter by the trio on the floor until they realized they had a visitor; then they grew silent.

Near the window, Mrs. Keaton sat with young Wesley upon her lap. The smile dropped from her face and she uttered, "Emily," in a strained tone.

Miss Collins sat up and gazed at him from her position on the floor, her blue-and-white skirt billowed out around her. Without the least hesitation she politely said, "Good morning, Lord Hawksworth."

A quick inspection of the children showed not a single red spot on any of their rosy cheeks. Fury almost choked Oliver as he realized what the lady had done. She had driven his guests away with a false tale of illness.

"Nursing the children back to health, Miss Collins?" the earl said with contempt.

A slight flush came to the lady's cheeks as she rose. Without answering his question, she got Honoria and Jamie settled at a table with paper and a box of water colors, then requested each to paint a picture of what they liked most about England.

Oliver watched as she went to a desk near the fireplace and picked up the birdcage, which was uncovered and revealed one red and one green parrot. With her eyes straight ahead, she walked past him into the hall. She signaled Swarup to stand back as the servant moved to take the cage from her. With single-mindedness, she marched some distance down the hall, then turned to face him. The look on her face was one of polite inquiry. "You wished to speak with me, sir?"

At that moment Oliver's fondest wish was to throttle this annoying female. How dare she come to Hawk's Lair and completely disrupt all his plans?

While his contemptuous gaze swept her as she stood holding the squawking parrots, his ever-rakish self was suddenly struck with the notion that she looked quite different than she had the night before. There was a deliciously unkempt quality to the brown curls which had sprung loose from their top knot and now framed her oval face. Her cheeks, flushed from the children's game, held the hint of a blush. But what struck him most was the inviting moistness of her full pink lips.

The awareness of her as a desirable woman jolted him. He'd been prepared to rage at the drab entity of the night before, not this enticing female. With an effort, he tried to keep his mind on the matter at hand, but the lady looked so adorably provincial as she stood holding the cage that he found it difficult to concentrate.

That stirring of attraction reminded him that despite her trick to rid the house of his guests, she was not responsible for his new burden even though she had delivered them. Still, he deserved an explanation for her outrageous falsehood to his guests.

"Why did you misinform my guests regarding the children having the measles?"

"My lord, you have responsibilities now. For the present you have no time to be entertaining . . . well, to give it to you without the bark, sir, nodcocks and coxcombs."

"Nodcocks and coxcombs!" the earl sputtered angrily. He knew a sudden urge to defend the gentlemen, then halted, for in truth, the description fit the departed men exactly.

"As I said, my lord, nodcocks and coxcombs. There is much to be done to make certain the children are settled comfortably. I did what you should have done last night and that was to send your guests about their business in as polite a manner as possible." Emily knew she'd gone beyond what was proper, but sometimes it took drastic measures to make people see the error of their ways.

His lordship's eyes grew an icy blue. "Madam, not since the day my stepmother departed this world have I encountered a more managing female. Nor one who was harebrained enough to think I would allow her to direct my life."

"You flatter yourself, my lord. I have no interest in your life except as it pertains to these children. Within a matter of weeks, you may return to town and pursue your hedonistic delights as you see fit, but at this moment your full attention is needed here. Jamie, Honoria and Wesley have no mother or father in England to protect and love them. They only have you, who appear far more interested in your own amusements and your friends than your wards."

Her strong words were like having a glass of cold water dashed in his face. Except for his attempt to hire someone to take command of the children, he had given little thought to them. Still, who was this female to be giving him a setdown for his conduct? "Miss Collins, I am—"

"Awk! Nodcocks and coxcombs!" the green bird squawked from the cage.

The earl halted, momentarily distracted from what he'd been about to say. As he glared at the children's birds, he was struck by the fact that all the lady had said was true. He had been more concerned with going to a mill with his guests than giving his brother's children more than a passing thought. Too long concerned with only his wishes and desires, he'd been more interested in getting rid of this managing female who was disrupting his life than with putting his mind to what was best for his wards.

Flooded with guilt and disconcerted to see his own failings, he gave a terse laugh. The lady was making him aware of a side of himself that he didn't much like. For some unexplained reason, he also didn't like that she perceived him as selfish and uncaring.

"Awk! Nodcock!"

Seeing Miss Collins bite her lip in an effort not to laugh, the earl relaxed and enjoyed the absurdity of the parrot echoing their conversation. He allowed his laughter to become full-bodied and jovial.

Emily watched with relief at the earl's growing mirth at Janus's interruption. She was amazed at how humor softened the lines around his mouth, making him far more accessible than before. She could see why he'd had so much success with women.

"Miss Collins, I must again ask you to forgive my uncertain temper, but mostly you must forgive my neglect of my brother's offspring. I fear I have need of a female's knowledge to guide me in such matters."

"So you do, sir. Have the children no other living female relation?" Emily held her breath. She wasn't ready to leave Hawk's Lair so soon, although she tried to tell herself it was all about the children, and had nothing to do with the handsome man in front of her.

"Indeed, they have a great-grandmother living north of London." But as Oliver spoke of the dowager, he knew the last thing he wanted was to have the lady at the castle nagging him to marry Lady Cora at once for the sake of the children. Better that he should make use of the managing Miss Collins's knowledge of child care than subject himself to his grandparent's badgering on the topic of matrimony. "I shall write to my esteemed grandmother and invite her down once I have the children properly settled. But I fear worrying over the children at her age would be too strenuous. Would you be willing to help me?"

A sense of satisfaction surged through Emily. She'd gotten her wish. His lordship was at last focused on the matter at hand. "I should be delighted. The first thing

I would recommend is that the nursery and the adjoining bedchambers be repainted and refurnished, and that new books be purchased to instruct the children in a full variety of subjects."

The earl nodded.

"Their pets, Janus and Juno, need a large permanent cage in a chamber where there is always certain to be a fire. I would suggest the library."

"My library!" The earl frowned as he eyed the colorful birds.

" 'Tis certain to always be the correct temperature, for they are exotic birds and used to warmer climes."

Oliver wasn't certain how he would like having a noisy pair of parrots in his private sanctuary, but if they became bothersome, he would have them moved after Miss Collins had departed. All that mattered for the moment was getting the lady before him satisfied with the children's situation, so she could go on her way. "Is that all?"

"That will do for now, my lord. No doubt I shall think of other things which the children have need of as we go along." The lady thrust the cage into his hand. Then she turned and hurried back towards the nursery. When she reached the door, she turned and looked back at him with a saucy smile. "I shall remove the children to our sitting room while you get the workmen started in the nursery. Pray, don't dawdle, my lord. The children are most eager to get settled in their own rooms. Good day, Lord Hawksworth."

The lady then entered the nursery. Oliver stood speechless, holding the cage and staring at the spot where he'd last seen Miss Collins. What had just happened to him? He had come up here to give the lady a set-down for sending his guests away, yet she'd managed to turn the tables. Here she was giving him orders not to dawdle like a mere servant.

With a bemused shake of his head, he chuckled at the thought of how the mighty had fallen in the course of a few minutes.

"Awk! Nodcock!" The green parrot seemed to be speaking directly to Oliver.

"I was thinking the same thing about myself, old boy." With that, the earl turned and made his way back towards the library. He promised himself not to let Miss Collins get the better of him in their next meeting, yet he knew that some part of him was looking forward to that encounter.

Four

Lord Hawksworth marched into his library and unceremoniously dropped the birdcage on his desk. The parrots responded to such careless treatment with a chorus of squawks and flapping wings. Colorful bits of feathers went flying from the cage.

Sir Ethan, disturbed by the clamor of the birds, peered round the wing-back chair from his position by the fire. He grinned at the expression on Hawksworth's countenance as he glared at the caged creatures. The baronet was reasonably sure he knew who was responsible for that look of annoyance.

"Trying your hand at gamekeeping, Hawksworth?"

"If Miss Collins has her way, yes. It seems that my earldom is nothing in that lady's eyes. She practically ordered me to bring these birds to *my* library, which she has deemed to be the best place in the castle for them to reside. Why, she even instructed me to make certain they have a larger cage as well." The earl knew that he was doing it a bit too brown, but the lady seemed intent on taking control of his household.

The baronet rose and came to inspect the brightly hued parrots. He tapped the wicker cage and said, "Greetings and welcome to your new home."

"Awk! Nodcock!"

Sir Ethan gave a shout of laugher. "I cannot help but like such an impertinent lad or lass—whichever our talking feathered friend may be."

Hawksworth arched one dark brow. "Then you must greatly admire Miss Collins, for she has more impertinence than Prinny himself. I was just informed I must not dawdle in my duties to my wards. She insists on having the entire nursery floor refurbished, and as soon as may be."

The baronet bit his lips in an effort not to laugh. He was certain his friend had never encountered a beautiful young female resistant to the famous Carson charm. While he liked the earl excessively, Sir Ethan was not blind to his lordship's faults. Had one been looking for a person to be guardian to their offspring, Lord Hawksworth, dedicated as he was to his own amusement, would be the least likely person one would choose. It wasn't that the earl was cruel or selfish, but merely that he'd grown accustomed to having to please no one but himself. There could be little doubt that, with Miss Collins's help, the earl was about to be shaken from his old lifestyle.

"Do you wish to postpone our trip to observe the mill in Marksbury?"

"Not in the least. If Miss Collins wishes to take control of all matters pertaining to the children, then I shall leave her to it."

The baronet made no comment, but he was certain the earl would pay for his abandonment of the lady and the tasks she had outlined.

Oliver tugged angrily on the bell rope and awaited Bedows. His thoughts were in turmoil after the encounter with Miss Collins. He might momentarily need her wisdom about what was best for his wards, but she was sadly mistaken if she thought he would personally oversee the work. He had plans of his own and had no intention of allowing them to be interrupted by her and her undertaking.

When the butler arrived, his lordship requested that his steward be summoned. Within a matter of some ten minutes, Mr. Grant appeared, battered felt hat in hand. He was a burly young man with tousled blond hair and a Yorkshire accent, who was quite unused to being summoned except at Christmas, when he would give an accounting of the estate.

Hawksworth gave the man orders to have the entire third floor completely cleaned and painted. If new furniture was needed, Mr. Grant was to order it from Bath. The earl informed the fellow that he was to be guided by Miss Collins, but he was most certainly not to let her orders overrule common sense. Lastly, the gentleman pointed to the birdcage and told Grant to find some kind of larger enclosure to house the creatures within and put it here in the library for the time being.

Satisfied he'd more than fulfilled his duty to his wards, Hawksworth announced to Sir Ethan that he was quite ready to leave for the mill. The gentlemen exited Hawk's Lair bound for Marksbury and an afternoon's entertainment.

Emily closed the door to the nursery and leaned back against the oaken surface. What had she been about to be so impertinent with his lordship, telling him not to dawdle? Had she gone too far? She knew she must be careful. She would find herself packed off to London if she pushed the gentleman toward his duty with too much vigor.

"Emily, what did Lord Hawksworth say about your little trick to frighten the other gentlemen away?" Delia whispered as she came to stand beside her mistress. Wesley was asleep in his cradle, and the older children were still hard at work on their watercoloring.

"He made no comment about the prank because Janus distracted him. I think he was a bit angry, but once he had a good laugh at the parrot's chatter, his mood lightened. He asked that we stay and help him settle the children comfortably in their new home. And since that is what I was hoping for, I agreed."

Delia eyed her friend with a frown as Emily moved to the table and began to compliment the children on their pictures. That they were to remain under his lordship's roof was not the news Delia wanted to hear. She knew from her own bitter experience how a young girl could fall victim to a handsome face, and few could rival his lordship's rugged appeal. Emily might think she could steer the earl into a close and loving relationship with the children, but a rake was more likely to dally with Emily than pay heed to his wards.

As much as Delia loved the children, she was well aware they were his lordship's obligation. In truth, he need answer to no one about his treatment as long as it was humane. Emily was only endangering herself and her reputation by staying to convince him to be a loving guardian rather than one who merely met the children's physical needs.

Delia moved to the table where Emily stood. "I cannot think remaining here the wisest of plans, my dear."

Emily looped her arm through her companion's and drew her to the window, saying, "I know you think Lord

Hawksworth might make unwanted advances, but I tell you, he barely seems aware I am a female except where it comes to my knowledge about the needs of his wards." That fact pricked Emily's vanity a bit, but she tried to push it aside. "Once the earl becomes better acquainted with his niece and nephews, I just know he will come to love them as we do. He won't totally abandon them to nurses and governesses. Then we shall take ourselves off to London and taste the Season."

Delia made no further attempts to dissuade Emily from remaining at the castle. The widow had long known that while the heiress might be young, she knew her own mind and had inherited her uncle's strong will as well as a definite sense of right and wrong. She was determined to see the earl and the children united as a family.

Calls from the children to come and see their finished pictures soon distracted Delia and Emily from their worries. Each of the young Carsons wanted to describe their works of art. There was a great deal of laughter at Honoria's painting of the pieman she'd seen in Plymouth, for he looked quite like a pie himself in the painting. Jamie exhibited a passable rendition of a naval flagship with a Jolly Roger flying above it. When questioned about the odd pairing, the young man declared that being a pirate would be more fun than being a mere admiral.

A knock sounded at the door, and it opened to reveal a man who introduced himself as Lord Hawksworth's steward, Mr. Grant. Emily was soon drawn into a discussion about paint, wallpaper, furniture and curtains.

Helping the children put away the watercolors, Delia still had fears for her young mistress. Her one hope was that once her letter reached Mr. Joshua Collins, he would take some action to let Lord Hawksworth know that Emily was not without protection.

Finished with her discussion with the steward, Emily suggested to Delia that they take the children to their sitting room for a light luncheon. Struck by a thought, she added, "Perhaps we could invite Lord Hawksworth and Sir Ethan to join us and make it something of a party."

Mr. Grant looked up from the note he was making after measuring the window. "Beggin' yer pardon, Miss Collins, but 'is lordship and Sir Ethan done gone to Marksbury to the mill what all the county's been talkin' about for the past week."

A mixture of anger and disappointment washed over Emily. The earl had barely asked her to stay and help with the children and she'd agreed, only to find he had no intention of lending his time or support. Instead he'd chosen to hie off to entertain himself and his friend, dropping matters entirely in his steward's hands with her to oversee.

Well, he might think he could avoid the children, but she was determined he would not. As Honoria and Jamie gathered what they wanted to take with them to the sitting room and Delia picked up the just-waking Wesley, Emily plotted her strategy to have the earl come face-to-face with his young relatives.

By the time the gentlemen returned from the mill, a fine afternoon's diversion which had gone a bruising twenty rounds, it was time to change for the evening meal. The earl was in a companionable mood. He even found himself looking forward to seeing Miss Collins and getting a chance to admire her shapely figure, fine amber eyes and kissable mouth. Only as an afterthought did he wonder what progress had been made on the nursery.

The earl poured himself a sherry while he waited in the Blue Drawing Room. He had been standing at the mantel only a few minutes, gazing into the fire and letting his mind ponder the lady from India, when the door opened. He turned to greet the new arrival, but the welcoming smile fell from his face. Miss Collins was accompanied by Honoria and Jamie.

"Good evening, my lord." Miss Collins led the children to the sofa directly in front of him.

The earl noted that the young ones had been dressed as if it were a special occasion. Honoria wore a simple blue satin gown with lace at the long sleeves and collar and a dark blue ribbon at the high waist. Young Jamie was in a short velvet coat and matching green knee pants. Both looked as nervous as pickpockets at the Old Bailey.

Despite being disconcerted by the unexpected arrival of his niece and nephew, Hawksworth swept an admiring glance over Miss Collins. She looked elegant in a simple white muslin gown worked with gold thread about the low-cut bodice, where creamy twin mounds rose to tantalize him. Her light-brown hair sparkled with glints of gold and was pulled back from her lovely face, then fastened with a white-and-gold clasp, allowing a riot of curls to dangle behind.

The delectable Miss Collins urged the children forward. When the trio reached his lordship, the lady gave an innocent smile. "I thought that this evening would be a good opportunity for you to get acquainted with your young wards since the nurse you hired to take care of young Wesley and Mrs. Keaton is still dressing."

"Oh, you did?" Hawksworth reluctantly drew his gaze from her pretty neck to his niece and nephew. Suddenly the lady's physical assets paled in comparison to her audacity at bringing his wards to the drawing room without his permission. He knew nothing about children and wished to keep it that way. Wasn't it enough that he'd allowed Miss Collins to turn his house upside down with squawking birds in his library and a steady stream of workmen? Did she have to force him to spend time with young people, when he hadn't a clue how to go on?

Jamie and Honoria sketched a bow and a curtsey respectively and chimed in unison, "Good evening, Uncle Oliver."

The earl cast Miss Collins an irritated glance before he gestured to the boy and girl. "Well, be seated and tell me what you think about England, since it is your first visit." The children went to the sofa and Miss Collins chose a chair facing them, smiling at the pair as if they were her own progeny.

Jamie shifted restlessly on the gold-and-blue damask furniture. As he eyed the gentleman, a complete stranger, he saw little to alleviate his fear. He wanted to take Honoria and run back to the comfort of the sitting room, but Miss Collins said he must get acquainted with his father's brother. The boy shot the lady a questioning look, then decided that for his sister's sake he must be brave. What did he think about his new home?

" 'Tis frightfully cold here, sir, even when the sun is shining."

Miss Collins nodded her approval at Jamie. Then she looked to the earl. "I told the children that you would make certain they had proper clothing for our English winters. I fear we are all sadly lacking in woolen coats."

"To be sure, my wards will have proper wardrobes." The earl cursed his thoughtlessness on the matter. Even he knew that India's climate required little winter attire. "I shall send for a seamstress from the village tomorrow."

The lady's brilliant smile sent a tremor of awareness racing through Hawksworth's body. He forced his gaze back to the children, telling himself that Miss Collins was not the type of female he generally admired.

Without much thought to the direction of the conversation, the earl remarked, "When the weather is warmer, Jamie, you might like to go to the river and fish where your papa and I used to when we were your age."

Honoria's blue eyes grew wide and she drew her hands to her cheeks. "You mustn't make Jamie go to the river, Uncle. It is full of dragons."

Jamie cuffed his sister on the shoulder. "They aren't dragons, silly. Only crocodiles, and I am not afraid."

Emily rose and went to sit beside the trembling little girl. She had been only a few years older than Honoria was now when she'd first arrived in India and knew what terrors the child must have suffered in the country. "Honoria, there are no crocodiles in England, only in the East Indies."

"Are you sure?" The little girl looked doubtful as great tears welled up her eyes. "Papa always said we were never to go the river alone."

"And so you shouldn't. But there can be no harm in Jamie fishing with his uncle." Seeing the doubtful look on the child's face, Miss Collins looked to Hawksworth for help. "There are no crocodiles in England. Ask your uncle."

The earl had no experience dealing with children's fears, but something instinctive in him told him to go to the child. He crossed the space, then knelt and took her fidgeting hand in his own larger one. "My dear child, as Miss Collins just told you, we have no crocodiles in this country. You must know that I would never allow you to do anything that might harm you, Jamie or little Wesley."

Honoria stared into her uncle's blue eyes, which reminded her of dear Papa. "What about tigers? Are there any tigers in your woods?"

The earl smiled at her. "Not a single tiger to be found, but you must promise me that you will not venture into the woods without Miss Collins or your nurse."

The little girl's head bobbed, making her black ringlets bounce. "And elephants, snakes or lizards?"

Hawksworth shook his head in disbelief. "Good heavens, child, have you encountered every frightening creature of nature?"

Emily and the children exchanged a knowing glance. "My lord, an Indian estate is not for the weak of heart or spirit. Encounters with the resident wildlife are often unavoidable."

The life the three of them had experienced was so far removed from what the earl had known, he almost felt envious. But that emotion was quickly extinguished when Miss Collins next spoke.

"My lord, I wish to show the children how different your estate is from their father's in India. Will you take them to visit your home woods? A brisk walk with the children tomorrow morning would be just the thing." The lady's amber eyes twinkled at him.

At once the children, long pent up in ships, carriages, inns and nurseries, expressed their delight in such a plan. Jamie spoke for them both when he cried, "Oh, yes, Uncle, a walk in the woods!"

The earl rose and moved back to the fireplace. It would be churlish to refuse such a simple request. He glared at the lady who had backed him into a corner. "While that is an admirable suggestion to ease your fears, I don't want the pair of you to be out in this weather until you have proper garments. Once fitted with warm coats and sturdy walking boots, I promise to take you *and* Miss Collins walking in the woods." There was no way he would allow the lady to abandon him with his wards as she had once before.

Sir Ethan and Mrs. Keaton made an appearance in the drawing room at that moment, having met just outside the door. Emily directed the children to bid their uncle and his guests good night. Then she announced she would return once she'd seen them safely under the watchful eye of the new nurse. With the spontaneity of the young, both children gave their uncle a hug before bidding everyone good night.

As she led the children upstairs, Emily smiled to herself. She'd seen the softening in the earl's eyes, if only for a moment, as he'd responded to the children's affection. The first meeting with his lordship had gone well, and now they had plans for a walk in the woods. Lord Hawksworth might not know it, but the children were beginning to wrap their little fingers around his heart as she had known they would. The only problem was, Emily was afraid that if she wasn't careful she might find her own heart in danger of being captured by a rake.

Five

After safely delivering Honoria and Jamie into the capable hands of Mrs. Waters, Emily returned to the drawing room and to her surprise experienced a congenial evening. His lordship offered no rebuke for her high-handedness in bringing his wards to him without his permission. Instead he was all that was pleasant, engaging in amusing banter with Sir Ethan as well as inquiring about the ladies' experiences and life in India. He offered information on a variety of subjects he thought might interest the newly returned travelers, such as new books in print and changes in the landscape of London.

By midnight Emily had retired to her bed certain that there was more to Lord Hawksworth than his reputation as a rake. With time and a little push on her part, no doubt he would soon form a loving bond with his niece and nephews.

But as with most circumstances in life, matters rarely proceed so smoothly. The following morning, Honoria woke long before the sun's golden rays had begun to brighten the day. She lay in the warm comfort of the large four-poster bed for some thirty minutes hoping someone would soon come, but at last the impatience of her six years drove her to rise.

She threw back the covers, slid down from the high bed and found her slippers, but in the dim pre-dawn light could not find her wrapper. As the cold began to penetrate the simple white muslin gown, she decided not to waste time searching for the garment. She went to the door and pulled it open. There were no servants moving about, so she dashed down the hall past Miss Collins's room to Jamie's, opened the door and entered.

Kali, dozing on the end of Jamie's bed, stood and wagged his tail at the sight of Honoria. She ignored the small black animal to climb the mounting stool, then shook her brother.

The boy rubbed his eyes, then realized who had awakened him. He sat up and yawned. "What time is it, Nory?"

"Don't know but I am hungry."

Jamie peered out the mullioned windows at the sky, which was beginning to grow pink. "Won't be time for breakfast for hours, you silly." But having said that, the boy realized that he too was starved. Dinner the night before had been some strange concoction with too many vegetables in a heavy sauce which Jamie thought tasted like leaves. He and Honoria had only moved the food around on their plates, devouring the crusty bread, then the custard that followed. It had not been a filling meal for the growing pair.

Honoria tugged at the sleeve of her brother's nightshirt. "Can we not go to the kitchens and find some bread, butter and honey or jam?"

Jamie scratched his head as he pondered such a daring move. Two days earlier he would never have dreamed of venturing about Hawk's Lair without Miss

Collins or Mrs. Keaton, but his uncle had been quite agreeable last night. Surely he would not object to two starving children getting a little something to eat as long as they didn't disturb anyone.

"Very well, but we must be quiet."

He tossed back the covers and donned the slippers his sister handed him. The pair tiptoed to the door; then Jamie stopped and looked at his dog, who stood on the floor gazing up at him expectantly. "Do you think we should take Kali?"

"To be sure. If we leave her here alone, she will bark and howl, waking the others." Honoria bent down and stroked the dog's furry head, which garnered her a lick on the hand.

With that decision made, the children slipped out into the hall and made their way downstairs in search of sustenance, their faithful companion trailing behind them. It took some time before they found the green baize door which signaled entry into the kitchens, but at last they entered a cavernous room with windows near the ceiling which cast just enough light by which to see.

Everything was in its place. Rows of copper pots were set neatly on shelves built into the wall. There were cabinets full of dishes standing on edge to display the lovely blue pattern. Two large fireplaces and assorted tables cleaned the night before stood empty.

Honoria gave a shiver as they looked about the unfamiliar room. " 'Tis cold in here. Can we not make a fire?"

Jamie felt very grown-up as he replied, "To be sure, for I often watched Bhava build the fire in the kitchen at home in Haora."

The pair walked past the first fireplace, which housed

a black range set into the alcove, and made their way to the open hearth, where a spit rack stood empty and clean in front of a great banked pile of ashes. Jamie held out his hand searching for warmth.

"Perchance there are a few embers still warm in there, and I shall not need to use the tinderbox." He very much hoped so, remembering Bhava warning him never to play with fire. "Help me put a log in to see if it will rekindle a flame."

Honoria eyed the spit rack in front of the fireplace doubtfully. It was empty of meat, but the many iron skewers and the large frame looked too heavy to move. Still, she had faith in Jamie.

She followed her brother to the wood box situated near the back door to select a nice sturdy log. Jamie pulled it out and Honoria took the opposite end; then they made their way back to the pile of ashes.

Jamie paused and eyed the rack thoughtfully, then looked at his sister. "What we must do is toss the log over the spit." With a forceful swing, they threw the wood over the iron rack so it would fall into the accumulated ashes. But they misjudged their strength and the log thunked against the top of the hearth and plummeted into the ashes at an astonishing speed.

As the log crashed into the remnants of last night's fire, ash shot outward in a gigantic explosion of soot as if blasted from a cannon. The shower of ash rained down all over the kitchen. The children were waving their hands and coughing as the particles fell and Kali began to bark in all the excitement.

At last the air cleared and Honoria opened her eyes, then gave a howl of laughter. Her brother's black hair looked grey, as did his face and nightshirt. Kali had fared little better, but a quick shake and a sneeze seemed to set all to rights for the dog.

Jamie blinked the ash from his lashes, then looked at Honoria, who was equally coated in grey powder. But instead of laughing, he wailed, "This is dreadful! We shall be punished for this. Uncle Oliver will never let me go fishing now."

Honoria, being the more practical one, simply shrugged her shoulders. "I do not think Miss Collins will be so very angry. She will make Uncle be kind, like she did on our first night at the castle when he was so very cross. After all, this was but an accident."

"But we should not have come," Jamie said sadly as he looked down at his hands, which were surprisingly free of soot due to the length of the sleeves of his nightshirt. He bit at his lip, knowing they had often gone to the kitchen at their father's plantation, but it somehow seemed different to do it at the castle.

Honoria, undaunted by the mess, gazed about her. "But we *are* here, so let us find something to eat." She marched around the nearest dust-coated table and found the door to the larder. Within a matter of minutes she announced the discovery of all the items they required— bread, butter and strawberry preserves.

Jamie hesitated but a moment before hunger won the day. "Well, if we are going to get punished for this visit to the kitchens, we may as well obtain the reward for our efforts."

Completely unaware that they were making sooty tracks in the larder, the pair brought their breakfast out and placed it on a small table as far from the scene of their crime as possible. They unwrapped the loaf of bread and discovered they required a knife. Jamie opened several drawers in the tables but found only towels and aprons.

Moving to the cabinet that housed the dishes, he tugged on the first drawer. It appeared to be stuck. He put all his weight behind his effort, and the drawer at last came free—completely free of the cabinet, spilling most of the silverware all over the soot-coated slate floor.

Jamie looked at the mess, then with a stoic, "In for a penny, in for a pound," he selected one of the knives that had remained in the drawer and hurried back to the table to slice and butter the bread.

Perhaps it was fortunate for the children that Martin and several other footmen were with Antoine when he arrived in the kitchen that morning and discovered that his domain had been desecrated. Upon entering the room and seeing not only soot and ash coating every surface, but silverware scattered about the floor, as well as his lordship's wards sitting at Antoine's table, the Frenchman fell into such a fit that Martin was convinced the frog cook would have a seizure and die.

In a flash of desperation, the footman sent Sam to summon Miss Collins so the children might quickly be removed from the Frenchie's sight. Nate was dispatched to awaken Mr. Bedows in the hope that the butler might manage the ranting Antoine. Martin could only hope that Bedows would appear first. Otherwise Antoine might do himself a harm at seeing a female in his kitchen.

Upstairs, a sharp knocking at her door woke Emily. The footman, in a rush of words, explained about the disaster in the kitchen and the presence of the children. Emily's heart plummeted. She'd been so pleased with last night's meeting, and now this! She requested that

Sam wake her manservant and have him come to her at once. Swarup might be needed if tempers flared in the kitchen.

With that she closed her door and quickly dressed in the first gown her hand touched, not bothering with her stays. Things were too desperate at the moment. She didn't put up her hair or don her stockings. She slipped her feet into her half boots and raced down the stairs.

She arrived in the large kitchen some five minutes after being summoned, Swarup right behind her. The chaos which met her eyes was far worse than she had imagined. She would not even hazard a guess as to how soot had gotten everywhere; she could only assume the children were involved.

As she surveyed the disaster, Antoine, a short, rotund fellow with long dark hair, came into view. He was ranting as he paced in front of the hearth. Kali was right on his heels, barking her displeasure each time the man came near the children and shook his fist. The other servants were standing back, fearful of the Frenchman's mood.

The remnants of the bread and jam on the table beside Honoria and Jamie told the tale. The children must have risen early and crept into the kitchen in search of food. How the place had become coated in ash was still a mystery, however.

Deciding she must do what she could to get things under control, Emily pushed her way through the crowd of footmen hovering at the door and made her way to the children.

She ignored Antoine, placing an arm round each child. "Do not be frightened. I am here. We shall see you safely through this misadventure." With that the trio turned to face the Frenchman, who'd halted both his ranting and his pacing to stare at Emily in horror.

Antoine pointed a trembling finger at her and demanded, "Who is zes *femme* that dares enter my *domaine?*"

Emily was uncertain how to reply, having no true status in the castle. She didn't want to jeopardize the children's fate by getting into a quarrel with his lordship's prized cook. But neither did she want this man to think he could terrorize and dominate the children.

"I am Miss Emily Collins, sir. I have come to return the children to their rooms." Thinking it best not to pay undue attention to this tyrant, she called to Martin as she led the children towards the door. "We shall need a great deal of warm water to bathe—"

"*Arrêtez!* You will not leave here, *mademoiselle*, until I, Antoine, have an explanation for zes . . ." The Frenchman had to search for the exact word in English. ". . . zes atrocity."

Emily was quite unused to being spoken to in such a manner by a servant. But for the children's sake, she tried to rein in her temper. "As you can see, there was an accident when the children came down to find something for breakfast. I do believe they owe you an apology, *monsieur.*"

Antoine began to bellow his abuse in French. It was clear an apology would not suffice, but Emily's French was so deficient that she was unable to discern what the fellow was saying.

Losing her patience, she stamped her foot and shouted, "Silence! I have had quite enough of your insolence to me and to his lordship's wards. You forget yourself, sir."

The Frenchman's face grew quite purple with rage. He

took several menacing steps towards Emily, but Swarup edged between the cook and his target. The Indian spoke not a word, but merely crossed his arms. Antoine halted but a moment, then unleashed a new round of abuse on the lady, shouting and waving his arms.

"What is the meaning of all this clamor?" Lord Hawksworth's words knifed through Antoine's tirade.

In the silence that followed, Emily turned her gaze to his lordship. He was fully dressed for a morning ride in a dark blue coat over grey buckskins, gloves and riding crop in hand. He looked amazingly handsome, but he was the last person she had wanted to see at the moment. She had hoped to get the children away from the kitchen before the earl learned of this disaster, but that was not to be.

In an instant, Antoine began to pour out his tale to his employer in rapid French. As his lordship's brows drew downward, Emily's heart began to plummet. What would he do? She could only guess, but she would defend the children's right to visit the kitchen. This was their home now, and they should be allowed to treat it as such.

Hawksworth sighed as he listened to the Frenchman's tale of coming into his spotless kitchen and finding complete disorder visited by his lordship's wards. The fellow was threatening to give notice if his lordship did not order all and sundry to stay out of Antoine's kitchen.

Miss Collins stood staring at him defiantly, her lovely brown hair tumbling in soft curls well below her shoulders. His grime-coated wards were clinging to her skirts, their trembling mouths showing red remnants of their feast. It was just as he had thought—his brother's children were going to completely disrupt his household if he were not careful.

The lady determinedly announced, "My lord, I don't know what your cook is saying, but the children merely came down to have some bread and preserves. I know the kitchen looks a mess, but surely it can be easily cleaned. I am certain there is a reasonable explanation if they might be allowed to speak."

" 'Twas an accident, Uncle," the boy blurted out, then drew back to the lady's skirts when his uncle's gaze settled on him.

Jamie's wide, frightened eyes gave Hawksworth pause. The boy looked so much like his father at that age that the earl was reminded of an incident when he and James had come to the kitchens to find bread and cheese along with a flask of water so they might spend the day in the woods near the river, only to break a dish while searching for what they needed. His stepmother had been much like Antoine, demanding all kinds of punishment. But for once his father had stood firm, saying there was no true harm and merely ordering the boys to stay out of the kitchen if they meant to break things. Lady Hawksworth demanded they send a servant for what they wanted, as was proper.

He hoped he might never be as unyielding as his stepmother, but he would not have his wards running wild all over the castle. Strict discipline would be the key. Once his niece and nephews were given a set of strict rules, no doubt things would run more smoothly.

"Miss Collins, see the children are properly cleaned up. Have them in the library at ten o'clock." Despite his best efforts, his tone sounded clipped and angry even to his own ears.

For a moment he thought that she intended to protest, but then she seemed to think better of arguing. With a surprisingly docile, "As you wish," the lady shepherded the children from the room, the small black dog and the large brown servant trotting behind.

With that Hawksworth turned his attention to his cook. The man had a smug look on his face, as if he'd won a battle. There could be no denying that the fellow was a true genius with food, but Oliver knew that he'd allowed the Frenchman far too much control in household matters. Hawksworth risked losing the finest cook in England, but things at the castle had permanently changed with the arrival of his wards. Antoine would have to go back to London.

"I would have a word with you, Monsieur LeBeau." When the earl finished telling the Frenchman what would occur, the pompous man left the room in a huff, raining muttered curses on all women and children.

Hawksworth ordered Bedows, who arrived moments after him, to summon Mrs. Tremont at once. The woman cooked for the castle staff when his lordship was in London. There would now be a full-time position at Hawk's Lair if she was interested. Also, maids were again to be employed—that news sent a murmur of excitement through the footmen. With a final order to clean the cursed place, the earl left determined to enjoy his morning ride with Sir Ethan.

Emily hadn't been surprised at the earl's angry response to the disaster in the kitchen. He had shown little tolerance for the children interfering in his household routine. She knew they were not out of the woods yet. They still had to face the gentleman's reprimand after Jamie and Honoria were bathed and dressed. She only prayed the punishment would not be too severe.

By nine-thirty she and Delia had the children, hair

washed and neatly dressed, sitting in the Blue Drawing Room awaiting the meeting with their guardian. Emily had changed to a sedate grey merino wool morning gown, trimmed with black piping. Her hair was combed into a simple chignon at her neck. She hoped she looked wise and responsible enough to dispense advice.

The ladies had brought down a game of Pachisi, a Hindustani board game, to distract the children from their worries about what their uncle would say about their little adventure. Honoria was fascinated with the painted shells used in the game, but Jamie listened carefully to the simple rules, determined to win.

The game had barely begun when the sound of carriages arriving at the castle drew the ladies and children to the front windows. Two post chaises with an excess of luggage strapped to their backs had come to a halt on the driveway below. Within minutes, the postboys had opened the doors to each of the vehicles, and the travelers stepped to the ground.

Emily and Delia could only gape at the sight of the four females descending from the carriages. There could be little doubt who and what the earl's visitors were.

A great deal of braying laughter and ribald comments about the postboys could be heard as the visitors inspected the castle. Due to the height of the drawing room windows, all the watchers could see of the females below were gaudy hats with an over-abundance of dyed feathers and garishly colored capes trimmed with swansdown, which were tied so as to expose a great deal of the callers' feminine assets to the world.

Delia's hand fluttered to her mouth as she whispered, "Surely Bedows will not allow those creatures entry."

Emily suspected this might not be the first time the castle had been invaded by light-skirts, for that was clearly what they were. Hawksworth was a rake after all. Anger at the earl began to well up inside her. Did he care so little for his young relatives that he would expose them to such women? Or worse, had he intended to merely lock the children into the nursery during his debauched revels?

She struggled to keep a rein on her growing ire. "No doubt they were invited to entertain his lordship's guests."

Honoria tugged on Emily's hand to get her attention. "How come you never wear such pretty feathers on your bonnets, Miss Collins?"

Delia quickly replied, "Ladies of quality do not need such vulgarly ornate adornments, my dear."

Emily, realizing the children were watching the arrival avidly, said, "Delia, would you escort Honoria and Jamie upstairs until his lordship's guests are sent on their way?"

Emily was determined to see that happen before the afternoon was well advanced.

"Are you not coming?" Delia asked in surprise.

"Not at the moment." Emily could not explain to her friend what she intended to do, for she wasn't quite sure herself.

Downstairs, Bedows's eyes grew quite round when he opened the door and discovered four birds of paradise chattering like magpies about the elegance of Hawk's Lair. The butler was well aware of the earl's reputation with women, but over the course of the last ten years, there had never been such vulgar females housed at the castle. The old man knew from his lordship's valet that Hawksworth as a rule did not dally with common actresses, preferring the willing ladies of Society.

But then the male guests invited to the castle on this

occasion, with the exception of Sir Ethan, had not been up to the earl's usual standards either. Perhaps his lordship had intended these coarse creatures to entertain Mr. Bonham and Mr. Abbot.

The old servant wondered if the earl had forgotten to uninvite these light-skirts after the arrival of his wards and the defection of his guests. Bedows was in a quandary. Should he usher the women into a drawing room or send them to the Red Lion in the village until his lordship could make other arrangements?

In truth, Lord Hawksworth had sent a message to the actresses not to come, along with ample compensation for their inconvenience. But unfortunately for Miss Colette Devereau, the missive had arrived during her performance at the Drury Lane Theatre. The manager of the small troupe of actors and actresses had intercepted the missive and pocketed the fifty pounds, hurrying to his favorite ale house. He'd disappeared without informing the actress that she and her friends would not be needed at Hawk's Lair. So the ladies had hired carriages and set out on the long, cold journey to Bath.

Bedows, hoping his lordship would return from his ride at any moment, opted to delay the women's entry. It just didn't feel proper to have these fancy articles in the castle when ladies like Miss Collins and Mrs. Keaton were in residence. In a voice that left no doubt of the superiority of his station in life, he asked, "Are you certain that you are expected, madam?"

The smile on Miss Devereau's face grew a bit brittle. "Of course we are expected. Do you think we have driven all the way to the country for our health, you silly old sod?" With that the three females behind her brayed with laugher. "Now stand aside, for his lordship is waiting."

The old retainer looked down his nose at the female with the painted face. "Lord Hawksworth is not at home this morning, madam. Mayhap you would go to the nearest inn and allow his lordship—"

"Go to an inn!" The actress put her red calfskin gloved hands on her hips. "Who do you think you are to be turning his lordship's *invited* guests away, you tallow-faced old—"

From behind the butler a female voice interrupted, "Is there a problem, Bedows?"

The butler gave the young lady a frown. "Nothing I can't handle, Miss Collins."

Emily scrutinized the women outside with interest. She had never been quite this close to such females, and she was truly curious what it was that the gentlemen saw in such flamboyant creatures.

Miss Devereau, seeing a woman inside the castle in a plain grey gown, jumped to the faulty conclusion that she was the housekeeper, albeit a very young one. But then, rakes were called rakes for a reason. "I have been telling this obnoxious fellow that we are invited guests of Lord Hawksworth."

Emily didn't know what possessed her, but she suddenly announced, "Then, Bedows, escort his lordship's guests to a drawing room to await the earl's return."

Bedows appeared relieved that Miss Collins had arrived to take the responsibility from his aged shoulders. "Very good, miss. This way . . . *ladies*."

He led the quartet of actresses to the Queen's Saloon, the finest chamber in the castle, hoping that the grandeur of the room would intimidate the creatures into a semblance of sedate behavior.

About to depart, he was startled when Miss Collins entered behind him and requested that refreshments be served. The old man cupped his mouth with a thin bony hand as he whispered, "Miss, you needn't stay with this lot. 'Tain't proper, nor would his lordship expect it."

Emily merely smiled, saying, "But I am interested in meeting Lord Hawksworth's guests." Placing a reassuring hand on the servant's arm as his worried expression deepened, she added, "Do not worry, Bedows. I am quite capable of managing things of an unusual nature."

As the butler left, he heard Miss Collins greet the loose females as if they were from the local church sewing society instead of the Haymarket ware they were. He shook his head, wondering what Lord Hawksworth would make of the gathering in the saloon upon his return.

Some thirty minutes later, Hawksworth and Sir Ethan cantered into the stable yard after a brisk ride about the earl's estate. Oliver was in a far better mood than he'd been when he left. At least he was reconciled to the loss of his French cook at Hawk's Lair, if not happy about the matter. There could be few house parties at the castle until the children were grown, and Mrs. Tremont's fare of simple but good English cooking would suit him during his brief visits in the future.

The earl was startled to see two strange carriages drawn up beside the paddock. His dark brows drew together as he looked at his friend. "What new catastrophe has arrived in my absence? I begin to think my life has suddenly become cursed by some evil demon."

Sir Ethan laughed. "Are you growing superstitious on me after all these years?" The baronet, recognizing the look of hired livery and the abundance of heavy luggage still strapped on the vehicles, suspected the identity of the visitors. "Perchance it is something simple. Did you forget about Miss Devereau and her companions' arrival?"

Oliver experienced a moment's discomfort at the thought of an assortment of singularly coarse actresses invading the castle with his wards and two females of quality in residence. "It cannot be. I assure you, I sent Colette Devereau a letter informing her of the change in plans and included ample compensation to soothe any actress's greedy little heart."

But a few moments' conversation with the postboys dashed the earl's confidence. Somehow there had been a mix-up, and Colette and her band of high flyers were now inside his home. With due haste, Hawksworth made his way to the castle.

On entering the front door, he was greeted by Bedows. Oliver immediately asked, "Where are they?" There was no need for him to explain to his servant who "they" were.

"In the Queen's Saloon, sir." The butler hesitated only a moment before adding, "Being served tea by Miss Collins."

"Good God! Was there ever a more troublesome female? Had she no sense of decorum?"

The earl turned on his heel without waiting for or expecting a response from either his butler or his friend to his rhetorical question. He marched straight into the Queen's Saloon without any warning to the room's occupants.

His gaze locked with Miss Collins's the moment he stepped through the door. A defiant light twinkled in the amber depths of her eyes, as if to warn him of her mood.

She calmly rose, dressed in the prim grey gown she'd arrived in. "Good morning, my lord."

Before he could utter a word of reproach to the lady for socializing with such low females, the ever-ambitious Colette, upon seeing his lordship, rose and dashed towards him, throwing her arms round his neck. "You have come at last, dear Hawk."

The cloying odor of the actress's perfume made the earl's stomach churn with revulsion. Or was it the heavy paint on her lips and cheeks he found so repellent? All he was certain of was that he found the woman completely unappealing as he pulled her arms away and set her from him.

"Did you not receive my message not to come, Miss Devereau?" His tone was cool.

Collette Devereau, being the daughter of a tanner, had very little education, but like most women in her profession, she did know men. Every line of his lordship's face was telling her she and her friends were an unwelcome sight. Did it have something to do with the pretty little chit who'd welcomed them into the castle? She watched the earl's blue gaze stray to where the young woman was seated, but there was more of an angry glint in their depths than lust. All she was certain of was that she didn't want to alienate the earl. He might not be interested at the moment, but one never knew when their paths might cross again.

"No, I did not, my lord."

The earl paid little heed to Miss Devereau. His gaze was again riveted on Miss Collins. Anger at her interference in his affairs drove him. He stepped around the actress even as he apologized.

"Sir Ethan will explain the misunderstanding and compensate you and your companions for your misspent time, but you must forgive me, for I have an urgent matter which I wish to discuss with Miss Collins."

Without another word, he went to the lady, took her by the arm and marched her from the company of the London light-skirts.

Six

No sooner had the drawing room door closed than Emily attempted to pull her arm from his lordship's firm grasp. But his strength was considerable, and he held her tightly until he had guided her across the Great Hall and into the privacy of the library.

The earl released her arm as he taunted, "Miss Collins, have you taken complete leave of your senses?"

"Is there a problem, my lord?" Emily inquired with feigned innocence.

The earl's dark brows drew downward in a frown as he glared at her. "Do not play the henwit with me. I have been on the receiving end of your pointed comments enough to know you are not lacking in intelligence and can well see what those women are."

Emily straightened the sleeve of her gown, brushing out the wrinkles the gentleman had inflicted. "What those women are, sir, are your invited guests." She looked boldly into his blue eyes, and asked, "Would you have them sent away without any refreshments after their long, cold journey at your request?"

"I would not, but neither would I have expected *you* to be acting as hostess in my absence." There was a slight upward tilt to his firm mouth as he seemed to realize he'd landed a blow to the lady's pride.

Emily blushed as his remark struck home. She had been out of line to assume such a role. But never would she admit as much to the man who had summoned such females into the very home which housed his wards.

Determined not to give an inch in the argument, Emily airily said, "Pray forgive my putting myself forward in such a manner, my lord. But Bedows seemed to be at something of a loss to have such women in Hawk's Lair. I fear his principles were getting in the way of your amusement." The audacious twinkle in the earl's eye was too much for Emily to bear. "But then, rakes are not known for paying much heed to principle, are they?"

In an instant, Emily realized she had over-stepped the bounds of civility as well as those of decorum. Every line of the earl's body went rigid. "Miss Collins, you go too far."

A little fearful of the dark look in his lordship's eyes, she distanced herself by moving to the nearest window. She pushed aside the green velvet curtain and looked out at the garden. Not wishing to be thought ill bred, she attempted to justify her conduct. "If I have done so, my lord, you must blame it on my desire for your niece and nephews to have the best of circumstances in their new home. They have lost so much at such tender ages."

"And you think I don't wish for the same?" The earl's tone remained angry, but there was a bit of wounded pride there as well.

Emily dropped the curtain back in place as she turned to face his lordship's understandable ire at her meddling. "Your conduct over the past few days has been anything but reassuring as to the priority you place on the children, sir. The arrival of such females was just—"

"A miscommunication, Miss Collins." The earl put out his hands in a gesture of entreaty, as if determined to make her understand. He gave a discouraged sigh as he dropped them to his side in frustration, then came to where she stood. The anger was gone, and in its place was a look of earnestness.

"Immediately upon my wards' arrival, I sent a letter requesting that the women not come. You may think me a care-for-nobody, Miss Collins, but I do have principles."

With all his pride and ire gone, Emily found Hawksworth frighteningly appealing. His dark gaze seemed to capture her own and insist she believe him. She realized that despite his reputation as a rake, there might be deep within him a voice of honor trying to tell him what was correct, at least where the children were concerned. Unfortunately, she was afraid that it was buried so deep under that polished, self-indulgent exterior that he might never heed its call.

As his compelling blue eyes seemed to draw her to him, Emily realized that her own heart might make her vulnerable to this practiced rake. In his mind she might be merely another female to conquer—a conquest to charm, then seduce and abandon. She knew that was how men of his stamp behaved, but still the thought brought a strange ache that the man was so trifling.

She must be on her guard. In a voice a bit shaky with emotion, she glibly said, "A rake with principles—what a novel idea." She walked round him towards the door, needing to get away from his powerful spell. As she reached for the handle, she glanced back to see a puzzled expression on his handsome face. Remembering the unsavory tales about him, some imp seemed to drive her onward. "A rake's principles? Do you suppose that is something like an ostrich's wings, sir? The great bird knows they are there but never bothers to use them."

Hawksworth stood frozen by the window as the door clicked shut behind Miss Collins. He mentally ranted and raved not only about the lady's audacity in welcoming the actresses but her insult to him. He had principles. Were his tenants not well cared for? Were his properties not well maintained? Had he ever done harm to any human or animal? The moral questions continued to come, but when he asked himself about taking into account the wishes and needs of others, he found it more difficult to give satisfactory answers. Over the course of the years there had been women whom he'd used, then tossed aside when he'd grown tired of them without the least thought to what they wanted.

It was in that reflective mood that Sir Ethan found Lord Hawksworth some ten minutes later.

The first words out of the earl's mouth were, "I tell you, I should send that Miss Prunes and Prisms packing to London, no matter the service she has rendered my family by returning my wards to England."

The baronet, fully expecting his lordship's indignant mood after finding Miss Collins closeted with such low females, knew the gentleman needed some time to recover his good humor. Sir Ethan walked up to a table which held a bowl of fresh fruit and picked up a bunch of hothouse grapes. Then he moved to where the parrots' cage sat on a pedestal near the fireplace.

"I assume you are referring to Miss Collins?" He plucked a grape from the bunch and offered it to the red parrot, hoping his friend's temper would subside and allow his intellect to control his actions.

Hawksworth moved to stand beside the Scotsman as he fed the birds. "Yes, she dared lecture me on my apparent lack of principles. The lady seems to think I might not be interested in what is best for my wards."

The baronet arched one auburn brow as he pulled another grape free and fed the green parrot. "Are you so angry because you think perchance she may be correct, or because you do not like such a pretty lass not falling prey to your charms?"

The earl made no comment as he watched his friend. But he suspected there was some truth to his ire being partly caused by the lady's indifference. It was clear she didn't see him as agreeable or charming, only as a failure at doing his duty. He wasn't quite certain why, but he wanted her to respect, even admire him, despite her tendency to lecture him.

Was she correct? Was he failing to do his best for his wards? The earl was interested in the baronet's opinion. "Do you think I'm not being a proper guardian?"

"Shouldn't be asking an old bachelor like me, laddie." Sir Ethan plucked the final grape, then tossed the empty stems into the fire. After giving the treat to Janus, the gentleman turned his curious gaze on the earl. "But 'tis plain that the ladies seem to think you need to do a bit more with the wee ones."

"More? What more?" The earl was genuinely puzzled. "I rarely saw my father except at Christmas until I was older. Then my brother and I were occasionally allowed to join him while hunting. What do they expect me to do?"

Sir Ethan, having had private conversation with Mrs. Keaton during dinner, was well informed of what Miss

Collins wanted. But the baronet was not sure his friend was the type of man who would adapt well to the demands of children, having been raised by a cold and distant father.

Still, he decided to lay out the matter for Hawksworth. "I believe what would make the lady happy is for you to become better acquainted with the children and make them feel welcome in their new home."

The baronet laughed at the expression of trepidation which settled on the earl's face. "Afraid you will be brought to grass by your brother's spirited offspring?"

The earl cracked a half smile for the first time since he'd entered the library. "Very likely, for I haven't the least notion what would be expected of me."

Remembering his lively nieces and nephews in Scotland, Sir Ethan grinned. "They like nothing more than an adult who will join in their fun. I don't believe it is hard to participate in such simple sports. All you require are the abilities to run, jump, shout, sing, ride and play games."

Hawksworth slumped down into a nearby chair. "Is that all? Sounds as though exercising my principles is going to be excessively tiring."

Emily closed the door to her bedroom, then walked over to the window to stare out. What was the matter with her? She was here to help the children, not to become addlebrained over Lord Hawksworth, for that was the only way she could describe her conduct in the library.

Delia had been right. There was danger in staying in a rake's residence. Despite her best intentions, she was finding herself unable to resist his attraction. But even worse, she was no closer to getting him to truly care for his wards than on the night of their arrival.

Perhaps she was on a fool's errand. His lordship might be too set in his raffish ways to make room in his life for the children. To be honest, after hearing the conversation between Lord Hawksworth and Miss Devereau, it was clear that the earl had attempted to stop the females from leaving London. On that head at least, she was convinced there was not likely to be a repeat of such inappropriate visitors in the castle.

Still, what the children needed most was someone to take as much interest in their lives as a parent. That was where her doubts about the earl lay, and she saw no simple solution.

A knock sounded on the door which led to the sitting room. At Emily's call, Delia entered, looking at her closely. "Have you quarreled with Lord Hawksworth once again?"

Emily shook her head and walked over to the dressing table. She picked up her brush and began to smooth down the curls which had sprung from her chignon. But her thoughts about her attraction to the earl still bothered her. "Not exactly a quarrel, more an exchange of opposing ideas."

Delia came to stand beside her friend. The bemused look on the girl's face reflected something that frightened the widow. Was Emily becoming enamored with his lordship? That might only lead to disaster. Delia knew she must do something.

"May I offer an observation, then a suggestion?"

Emily, pushing her worries aside, ceased fussing with her hair and smiled at her companion. "Of course."

"I think your unusually close relationship with your uncle has given you a somewhat unrealistic impression of the role of a guardian. Mr. Ashton, having no children of his own, treated you as a beloved daughter, but most orphans are lucky to have a roof over their heads and enough to eat. Lord Hawksworth will generously provide for the children's physical needs and, given time, he might even develop an affection for them."

Emily frowned. "Time! He is likely to forget about them once he returns to his—"

Delia raised her hand. "And so he is, for most men would forget their heads if they weren't attached, but I have a suggestion which will give the children exactly what you think they need."

With a wicked grin, Emily inquired, "Does it involve chains and the castle basement? I am convinced that is all that will keep Hawksworth near his young relatives."

"In truth, it doesn't involve the earl, but us."

Emily's gaze dropped to the hand which still held her silver brush. How could she tell Delia that staying at the castle was not a possibility that Emily would consider. She knew herself to be in danger of the earl's appeal and was no longer certain of her ability to resist. "As much as I should delight in remaining with the children, I cannot think his lordship is willing to offer us long-term hospitality." Especially after she questioned his principles.

"We need not remain at Hawk's Lair to see the children. Back in India, you said you wanted to lease or purchase a small estate in the countryside. Why not near the castle? I am certain his lordship would not deny us the opportunity to visit with Honoria, Jamie and Wesley."

A smile lit Emily's face. She tossed the brush on the dressing table, then hugged her friend. "That is a wonderful suggestion. I have been so busy trying to get

Hawksworth to take an interest, that I never thought about us maintaining contact. I shall begin to look for a suitable place tomorrow."

A knock sounded at the door. Emily called for the visitor to enter. Martin opened the door and announced that his lordship had summoned the village seamstress, Mrs. Nance, and the lady was wishing a word with Miss Collins and Mrs. Keaton in the rear parlor before Nurse brought the children.

As the ladies made their way to meet the woman, Delia said, "See, I think you underestimate his lordship's concern about his wards. Why, 'twas only last night that you mentioned the children's need for warmer clothes and here is Mrs. Nance."

Emily shook her head. "I never doubted he would see to their material needs, my dear. It's their emotional well-being I am worried about, but your suggestion of our remaining in the neighborhood has greatly calmed my fears about that." She told herself it didn't matter if the earl returned only rarely to the castle, for now she and Delia would be close at hand. But the thought of not seeing the earl again left her surprisingly melancholy.

Putting her thoughts about his lordship aside, she followed Delia into the small parlor at the rear of the castle. Emily discovered Mrs. Nance to be a tall woman with a plain face and bright red curls, who wore a fashionable blue wool gown of exceptional cut. It was apparent that while the seamstress might live in the country, she owned a superior skill in her craft.

After introductions, the seamstress announced, "His lordship says I am to be guided by you, Miss Collins, as to the children's needs. I took the liberty of bringin' a few ready-made items, since I heard the little ones are recently returned from the Indies."

The woman opened a trunk and took out several woolen jackets in varying sizes. She announced that the garments had been sewn for the local squire's sons, but as they were in London at present, mayhap one might fit the earl's eldest ward. "For it is certain I am that the young lad is anxious to be out of doors, even though it's been colder than a woodsman's nose in winter this year."

Delia selected one of the grey jackets, saying, "I think this would fit Jamie exactly." Then she lowered the garment and looked at Emily. "You do realize that the moment the children have warmer coats, they shall be demanding an outing?"

"I am not afraid of a little cold weather." What Emily truly feared was an encounter with Lord Hawksworth after her loose tongue in the library. How could she have been so foolish as to question the man's conduct?

The business of outfitting his lordship's wards soon took precedence over her worries. She found herself liking the practical Mrs. Nance, and while the children were sent for to be measured, the three women put their heads together and drew up a list of the necessities.

By the time Bedows announced nuncheon to the ladies, Honoria and Jamie each had suitable attire for the cold Somersetshire weather. The other garments would have to wait until Mrs. Nance and her assistants worked their magic with needle and thread.

With a promise to take the older pair for a walk after their meal, Emily set out with Delia for the dining room with some trepidation. As the servant opened the door, her heart hammered in anticipation of meeting with the earl, but to her relief, there were only three places set

and Sir Ethan there to greet them. The baronet offered
the ladies the earl's compliments, informing them that
his lordship had gone to Bath on business with his steward.

Sir Ethan proved a companionable host, but Emily
was not in a talkative mood. As he conversed with Delia, the young heiress allowed her mind to return to the
earl. She knew she must now repair the damage she
had done with her insulting gibe. She owed Lord
Hawksworth an apology. Upon his return she would
seek him out, but the thought of being closeted alone
with the gentleman sent a tremor of excitement racing
up her spine which, despite her efforts, she could not
dispel.

That afternoon a blustery wind swirled around Emily,
her two lively charges and Kali as they explored the
grounds of Hawk's Lair. Having taken Bedows's advice,
they'd exited through the north portico into a well-
maintained knot garden where remnants of snow remained only in the shadows of the tall shrubs. The
children were delighted with the six intricate knots
which surrounded a lovely center fountain. They each
chose a separate knot and began to dash about inside
the knee-high sculpted bushes, attempting to reach the
center first. The small black dog ran back and forth
between the pair and barked playfully.

Emily, left to her own devices, took her first look at
the exterior of the castle in the light of day. It was a
building of mellow brick and interesting design with numerous domed turrets. She was certain that if she possessed such a splendid home, she would never wish to
leave it.

Just then Jamie called that there was a gate into another garden. The trio, with Kali trailing, passed through the ornate iron portal to explore a lower garden with ancient clipped topiary in a variety of shapes. In that manner they spent the afternoon venturing into new terrain and enjoying the delights of the estate.

Nearly an hour later, Honoria announced she was quite tired, but she begged to be taken to the stable to visit with Matilda before returning indoors. In a grown-up voice, she announced, "We must see that she is properly housed, Miss Collins."

Jamie was agreeable if it meant extending his time out of doors, so with directions from a passing gardener, they made their way to the complex of buildings at the rear of the castle where the goat now resided. As they approached the entry, Hawksworth drove up before the open door of the building in a high-perch phaeton. Emily's heart began to hammer. He climbed down and tossed the reins to a young groom, then fell into conversation with a man who appeared to be in charge.

Emily knew the exact moment he became aware of their approach. There was a perceptible straightening of his back. Her knees suddenly felt weak at the thought of facing his rancor, but she decided there was no use delaying her bad medicine.

"Good afternoon, my lord."

"Miss Collins," Hawksworth responded, his tone frosty. Then his gaze moved to the two children, who eyed him cautiously, and there was a softening in his frigid features. "I must say that I am delighted to see the pair of you looking much cleaner than when we last met."

Jamie glanced up at Emily; then, without the least encouragement, he tugged off his quartered cap and gamely stepped forward. Still, there was a slight tremor of fear in his voice as he spoke. "Uncle Oliver, Honoria and I wish to apologize for the dirt and disorder we caused in the kitchen this morning. Our only excuse is that we were excessively hungry, sir, but we promise never to intrude there again."

Hawksworth found himself touched by the lad's bravery. He wondered how his brother had handled the matter of disciplining the children for their transgressions. He couldn't imagine James being a hard taskmaster, having been so terrified of their father as a young man.

Drawing his hands behind his back, Oliver knew that he could not let such a serious offense pass without some mention. "Well, I hope that you and Honoria will in the future avoid any matters concerning fireplaces, but since I think you intended no harm we shall let the matter drop. I would suggest, however, that you summon a servant or your nurse in the future if you should wake and find yourselves famished."

"Yes, Uncle Oliver." Jamie dug the toe of his boot into the dirt nervously.

"What brings you to the stables?" Hawksworth asked the lad, but glanced up to see Miss Collins gazing at him. He took note that she worried her lower lip with even white teeth. Was the intrepid lady regretting her barbed comments in the library earlier? Or merely considering lambasting him further for his moral turpitude?

Jamie, unaware of the undercurrents from the adults and having been absolved of his crimes in the kitchen, peered into the shadows of the building that housed his uncle's prime cattle. Like most young lads, he was eager to inspect the interior of so fine a stable. "We came to visit our goat, Matilda. We want to make certain she is happy in her new home, sir."

Hawksworth signaled his head groom, who had moved away with the arrival of the children and Miss Collins. "Bates, take my wards to wherever you have their goat housed."

The craggy-faced fellow grinned at Jamie and Honoria, then gestured for them to follow. "Come this way, for I've got yer pet in the rear barn with the yearlin's."

Without the least fear of the old man, the two young Carsons dashed after Bates with Kali on their heels and soon fell into step with him as he led them down the aisle and through the rear doors of the barn. Hawksworth arched a dark brow when Miss Collins remained standing in front of him.

"Do you not wish to inspect Matilda's quarters as well?" There was a hint of sarcasm in his voice.

The lady's cheeks flamed pink. "I have no doubt that the children's goat is being properly cared for."

"So you think it only my wards I neglect."

Emily knew she deserved his disdain. "My lord, I . . . regret, er, that is I wish to offer you . . ." She struggled to find the right words.

The earl found himself enjoying her chagrin, but he was not a cruel man and took pity on her discomfort. "It *is* dashedly awkward, is it not?"

Emily gave an embarrassed grin; then her face grew sober. "It is, sir, but it must be done. I do regret my unkind remarks in the library and hope that you will forgive my unmitigated impertinence in criticizing the manner in which you conduct your affairs."

As the lady apologized, Oliver wondered what he found so intriguing about her. Clearly, she was not like any other female of his acquaintance, but then, those women had rarely intrigued him. He'd had little interest in getting to know any of the ones who'd satisfied his lust.

Miss Collins was headstrong and unconventional, yet she possessed a genuine concern for his wards. Her interests weren't solely centered on her own comfort and reward. He was certain his grandmother might wish that he would learn empathy for others from the lady. But he would learn little if they continued at odds with one another.

Realizing the lady had finished with her apology and was waiting expectantly for a reply, Oliver said, "I do believe the better part of our acquaintance has been spent in one or the other apologizing, Miss Collins. Do you think we might cry peace and start anew with the knowledge that we both want only the best for my wards, even if our vision of what that is differs?"

The lady smiled with such radiance that Oliver found it difficult to believe he had thought her plain upon her arrival. But then, she'd had little to smile about that first night with his implacable orders about what he expected of her.

Miss Collins extended her gloved hand, bringing him out of his bemused thoughts. "I think that an excellent notion, my lord."

She had a surprisingly firm grasp for a female. As she drew her hand free, she asked, "Shall we go find the children? We wouldn't want them to fall into mischief."

Oliver had only to remember the disaster in the kitchen which had cost him his French cook to realize the truth in that. He gestured her forward and they entered the stable, walking past a variety of horses. As the lady stopped to admire his lordship's prized stallion, Oliver, determined to make a new start with his guest, inquired, "Do you or Mrs. Keaton ride? I have been remiss in not offering to accommodate you."

Emily stroked the black horse's nose. "I do, my lord, but Delia is more comfortable being driven. Might I be so bold as to request the use of one of your vehicles? When time permits, I should like to drive round the local countryside, for we are both most anxious to once again see the English landscape."

Despite his best intentions, Oliver frowned. He was often known to comment disparagingly on the women in town who drove carriages in the park. They either drove timidly, obstructing traffic, or at such a spanking pace that the animals' mouths were subjected to a great deal of abuse when reined to an abrupt halt for the ladies to socialize with their friends, as was their wont.

"My coachman is at your service. All you need do is send word to Bates and you can be driven to wherever you desire."

"Oh, that won't be necessary, sir. I am quite capable of driving myself." Emily was no fool. Too often, she'd been confronted with gentlemen who doubted her abilities with the ribbons. As she watched the changing expression on the earl's face, it was clear their new pact of peace was about to be put to the test.

Hawksworth grew thoughtful, then announced, "Very well, Miss Collins, I shall inform Bates to make a vehicle available for you and Mrs. Keaton."

Just then the sound of Kali's excited barking and a shout echoed from somewhere behind the stable. The earl and Emily exchanged a worried glance, then hurried in the direction that the children had gone with the head groom.

The sight that greeted them on entering the yearling barn made Oliver's blood run cold. His young heir had

We'd Like to Invite You to Subscribe to Zebra's Regency Romance Book Club and Give You a Gift of 4 Free Books as You Introduction! (Worth $19.96!)

If you're a Regency lover, imagine the joy of getting 4 FREE Zebra Regency Romances and then the chance to have th lovely stories delivered to your home each month at the lowest prices available! Well, that's our offer to you and here's how you benefit by becoming a Zebra Home Subscription Service subscriber:

- **4 FREE** Introductory Regency Romances are delivered to your doo
- 4 BRAND NEW Regencies are then delivered each month (usually bef they're available in bookstores)
- Subscribers save almost $4.00 every month
- Home delivery is always **FREE**
- You also receive a **FREE** monthly newsletter, *Zebra/ Pinnacle Roma News* which features author profiles, contests, subscriber benefits, previews and more
- No risks or obligations...in other words you can cancel whenever yo wish with no questions asked

Join the thousands of readers who enjoy the savings and convenience offered to Regency Romance subscribers. After your initial introductory shipment, you receive 4 brand-new Zebra Regency Romances each month to examine for 10 day Then, if you decide to keep the books, you'll pay the preferre subscriber's price of just $4.00 per title. That's only $16.00 fo all 4 books and there's never an extra charge for shipping and handling.

It's a no-lose proposition, so return the FREE BOOK CERTIFICATE today!

Say Yes to 4 Free Books!

Complete and return the order card to receive this
$19.96 value, ABSOLUTELY FREE!

(If the certificate is missing below, write to:)
Zebra Home Subscription Service, Inc.,
120 Brighton Road, P.O. Box 5214, Clifton, New Jersey 07015-5214
or call TOLL-FREE 1-888-345-BOOK

FREE BOOK CERTIFICATE

YES! Please rush me 4 Zebra Regency Romances without cost or obligation. I understand that each month thereafter I will be able to preview 4 brand-new Regency Romances FREE for 10 days. Then, if I should decide to keep them, I will pay the money-saving preferred subscriber's price of just $16.00 for all 4...that's a savings of almost $4 off the publisher's price with no additional charge for shipping and handling. I may return any shipment within 10 days and owe nothing, and I may cancel this subscription at any time. My 4 FREE books will be mine to keep in any case.

Name _____

Address _____ Apt. _____

City _____ State _____ Zip _____

Telephone ( ) _____

Signature _____ RN119A
(If under 18, parent or guardian must sign.)

Terms and prices subject to change. Orders subject to acceptance by Zebra Home Subscription Service, Inc.
Offer valid in U.S. only.

A
$19.96
VALUE...
FREE!

No
obligation
to buy
anything,
ever!

AFFIX
STAMP
HERE

ZEBRA HOME SUBSCRIPTION SERVICE, INC.

120 BRIGHTON ROAD

P.O. BOX 5214

CLIFTON, NEW JERSEY 07015-5214

gone up into the hayloft and now sat perched on an open rafter, clinging to a beam which ran across the wide aisle. On the same timber sat two calico kittens watching the young lad with eager curiosity.

"Uncle Oliver, Uncle Oliver," Honoria called as she dashed towards them, her bonnet loose on her shoulders. " 'Tis all my fault. Jamie went to bring me a kitty and now he cannot come down."

Oliver was certain he'd never known such anxiety as he watched the lad rocking back and forth on the oak beam, trying to extend his foot back to the top of the wall. If his nephew fell to the cobblestone floor, there would be nothing to be done for him.

"Where is Bates?" Fear made his voice harsh.

Honoria's gaze was locked on her brother, but she hesitantly responded, "H-He told us to stay in the pen with Matilda while he went to make certain his lads weren't idling with the new milkmaid."

Oliver would take a strip off the old man's back later for his negligence, but he knew Bates was as unfamiliar with children as he was. For now he needed to get the boy down. He removed his coat and tossed it heedlessly over a stall rail. Beside him Miss Collins called, "Don't move, Jamie. Your uncle will be up to help you down."

The earl took the stairs two at a time and entered the hayloft. It took only a moment to determine how his nephew had managed to climb to his precarious location. Oliver scaled the wooden slats, scraping his Hessians in the narrow space never meant for climbing, to where the lad sat frozen in fear. "Take my hand, Jamie."

His lordship's ward seemed to find confidence in his uncle's calm voice. After one fearful glance at the distant floor, he stretched out his dust-coated hand and grasped his rescuer's.

Below, Emily held her breath. She watched the earl pull the boy to him, drawing him tight against his chest. Within a matter of minutes, the two were safely back down on the loft floor.

His lordship hugged the lad for a second longer. "Are you all right, Jamie?"

The boy merely nodded his head. Honoria dashed up the stairs and hugged them both. "Thank you for saving him, Uncle."

Emily felt her heart warm as his lordship gazed down at the pair and ruffled their dark locks. "I told you I would take care of you. Now promise me you will never do anything so foolish again."

"We promise, Uncle Oliver," the pair chimed in unison.

When the trio were once again standing on the cobblestone aisle, Miss Collins thanked him. There was a warm glow in her amber eyes that surprised the earl and gave his spirits a lift. But there was no time for private conversation as the children drew the lady to Matilda's pen. After some moments of admiring the goat, she announced that they'd all had enough excitement for one day. With that, she swept the children back towards the castle.

The earl shrugged on his coat as he watched his young relatives and Miss Collins disappear round the corner. Oliver wasn't certain when it had happened, but he'd actually begun to like those two mischievous imps. Was that what Miss Collins had been trying to bring about? There had been a look of pure delight in her amber eyes as she'd watched the three of them hugging in the loft.

Clearly the children were going to be a handful, but with Miss Collins's guidance, he was certain he would manage. But would the lady be at Hawk's Lair much longer? The thought that she would be returning to her own life and affairs left him feeling unaccountably dissatisfied. Could he cope with the children without her guiding wisdom?

Then he remembered there was to be a female in his life—Lady Cora. For almost the entire week, he'd managed not to think about the woman his grandmother had him practically betrothed to. He hardly knew her, so why did the very thought of her plunge him into such gloom?

At that moment, Bates returned to the barn, and Oliver put aside his concerns about Lady Cora to chastise his head groom for his carelessness. Afterwards, as he made his way to the castle, he realized that he was looking forward to spending a pleasant evening with the ladies and Sir Ethan. His grandmother would be all amazement to find him content with such provincial entertainment. But for the first time since reaching his majority, he found himself not longing for the delights of London after a week in the country.

Seven

The following morning found the residents of Hawk's Lair much engaged in their individual concerns. Lord Hawksworth, applied to by his steward, Mr. Grant, had left early to help settle a property dispute on the northern boundary of the estate. In the upstairs sitting room, Miss Collins was happily entertaining young Jamie and Honoria while Mrs. Keaton played with Wesley under the watchful eye of Nurse.

Only Sir Ethan was at loose ends after writing several letters to his various family members in Scotland. Thinking to enliven his morning, he went to join the ladies.

Once granted entry, his gaze was drawn to Mrs. Keaton as he announced, "The morning is too fine for such bonny lasses and bairns to be indoors."

Emily noted Delia's cheeks flame pink under the baronet's scrutiny and began to suspect that the widow, despite her avowals of never remarrying, was developing a tendre for Sir Ethan. Thinking to promote a match for her friend, Emily said, "That is true, sir. Would you be kind enough to escort Delia and the children round the gardens?"

The baronet reluctantly drew his gaze from the widow. "Are you not to join us then?"

"Not this morning. I have another matter I must attend to." Emily was determined to begin her search for property in the immediate area this very morning. She'd spent a pleasant evening in his lordship's company. He'd even had Nurse bring the children to the drawing room before they dined and laughingly told the tale of the mishap in the barn, but she felt certain that a rake would only be amused for a short while with such domesticity.

Sir Ethan eyed her a moment, but made no comment. Instead he was content to offer his arm to the lady of his choice. Within a matter of minutes, Emily found herself alone as Nurse took Wesley to the nursery and the rest of the party went to don coats against the spring chill.

Emily returned to her bedchamber and quickly penned a letter to the solicitor who'd been her uncle's man of business in London, informing him of her return and her wish to purchase a small house in Somerset. Once the missive was sealed, she went in search of Bedows to have it posted to Town. She discovered the butler in his lordship's library overseeing the placement of the new, larger cage designed for the parrots.

After the two birds were moved into their new home and the workmen left, she went up to the cage to inspect the structure. It stood as tall as a wardrobe and twice as wide.

"It is a very fine cage," she said, counting some ten different perches and two swings behind the thin wire bars.

"Aye, Miss Collins, his lordship rarely does anything by half. Was there something you wished?"

She handed him her letter, but just as she was about

to request it be posted, Janus squawked, "Awk, Miss Collins, awk, Miss Prunes and Prisms."

Emily felt her cheeks warm.

Bedows glared at the green bird. "Now, miss, you know the feathered beastie don't mean it."

"Of course I do." She had little doubt who had uttered the phrase in front of Janus, and *had* meant the slur. Her pride was pricked, but she decided to put the matter from her mind. Perhaps her drive in the country might put her in better spirits.

"His lordship offered me the use of a team and carriage. Would you send word that I shall be going out in some ten minutes?"

"Very good, miss."

She returned to her room and donned her warmest apparel with the help of the newly employed maid, Jane. Emily wore her blue wool habit trimmed with black velvet. At last ready, she summoned Swarup to accompany her. After setting a low-crowned black beaver hat at an angle over her brown curls, she made her way downstairs. Despite her pique with Lord Hawksworth, a surge of excitement raced through her at the thought of driving in the English countryside.

In high spirits Emily arrived at the stable, but once again suffered a wound to her pride. She discovered that instead of a team and curricle, Bates had put an aged cob between the shaft of an ancient gig. She had no doubt the order for such a modest equipage had come from the earl. The insult to her skill with the ribbons, coming as it did on top of the slur repeated by the parrot, sent all her good judgment flying.

"This will not do. You," she called to the young groom who was holding the vehicle in anticipation of her arrival, "unhitch this horse. Then go to the carriage house with my servant and bring out one of his lordship's curricles."

The lad's eyes grew round as he gazed at the oversized Indian, but he quickly did as he was bidden. Within some ten minutes, a neat black curricle stood with his lordship's team of greys strapped in the traces.

With a defiant toss of the train of her blue habit, she took Swarup's hand and climbed in, waiting only for the servant to fit his large form into the perch in the rear. Giving a smart crack of the whip above the leader's head, she bowled out of the stable yard and down the drive.

Hawksworth had spent a surprisingly entertaining morning in friendly argument with his closest neighbor in regard to the north boundary, which was marked by a small creek on both deeds. Over the course of the past ten years, the small tributary's banks had moved progressively north, according to Mr. Evan Fawkes, owner of the next estate, depriving him of some of his more fertile lands. After inspecting the area, Oliver determined that with the melting of the recent heavy snows, the stream had indeed moved north in some areas. But there were also points where it had moved southward onto his property. After riding the disputed line and much debate, the gentlemen had returned to Fawkes's manor and drunk a glass of claret, agreeing to leave matters as they stood for the present.

The problem handled, the earl tooled his curricle along the road towards his estate, but as he came over a rise, he drew his team to a halt to admire the beauty of the Somerset countryside. Gazing fondly at the Mendip Hills in the distance, which glinted with a blue tint in the sunlight, Oliver wondered why it was that he spent so much time in smoke-filled London. Just then a flash of movement drew his attention to his left.

At the bottom of the hill stood a man, a white turban on his head, holding a team of horses drawn up beside the road in front of the rundown Broomfield Cottage. He recognized Swarup at once, but what puzzled him was that Miss Collins's man stood at the head of—damnation—at the head of Hawksworth's greys! Was Bates all about in the head to have defied orders and given one of his best teams to a female? Then he realized there could be little doubt of who had made the switch.

With a snap of the reins, Hawksworth put his team into a bone-jarring gallop, starting down the hill towards the servant and waiting carriage. Too concerned about his team, he gave little thought to where Miss Collins was.

Approaching the curricle, the earl furiously realized he had little choice but to allow Miss Collins to drive the team back to the castle, as he had no tiger with him. He reined his team to a halt just as the lady stepped through the arbored gate of the abandoned cottage. She paid little heed to him as Swarup aided her to step into the vehicle.

She took the ribbons in hand before she turned and smiled rebelliously. "Good afternoon, my lord."

"Miss Collins, what is the meaning of this? I left instructions you were to be given the gig and Old Belle." Even as he spoke, his expert eye scanned the state of his greys but found nothing untoward in their condition.

"My lord," Emily replied sweetly, despite the glitter in her amber eyes, "I was certain there must have been some mistake, for *old* Belle looked as if she was done for even before we started. I ordered something more suitable."

"Madam, there are no females of my acquaintance who have the skill to handle a team of this calibre. Pray return them to the castle at a sedate pace without doing them any further harm."

Two red warning flags appeared on Emily's cheeks, but her tone was polite. "I shall return them . . . at my own speed, my lord, and you can be certain they will be unharmed."

With practiced expertise, she cracked the whip and set the curricle at a spanking pace, leaving a cloud of dust in her wake. Hawksworth, furious at her defiance, set out after her, muttering curses about women trying to drive carriages. He determined to overtake her, then slow his curricle to block her path, but the gentleman had not reckoned with the lady's skill and the obstacles in his path.

The two vehicles barreled down the road towards Hawk's Lair. The greys were an excellent team, but his chestnuts could overtake them easily on a regular pike. But this was a simple country lane, barely wide enough for one carriage. To Oliver's frustration, he had to merely follow in a cloud of choking dust. The road they traveled twisted and turned, allowing the earl to watch the lady's skill as she passed a hay cart and then guided the team in full flight through the narrow bridge near the village without so much as scratching the paint. With that daring maneuver, Oliver experienced a revelation. He had no idea who had taught the young lady, but he knew he must own that she drove to an inch.

Miss Collins slowed the carriage and turned smoothly through the gates at Hawk's Lair. She allowed the team to come to a cooling walk up the drive, guiding the curricle back to the stables. She was standing on the ground with a defiant smile as Oliver drove up. He knew he owed her an apology, for her abilities with the ribbons could rival that of most of the gentlemen of his acquaintance.

Before he could utter a conciliatory word, she dropped her gaze to his driving cape. "Oh, I do apologize, sir. I did not intend for you to eat dust."

There was a twitch in her pink lips as she attempted not to smirk.

"I am sure you did not. I believe it was crow you were hoping I would eat after watching you drive. And so I shall. Will you accept my humble apology and allow me to say your driving is bang up to the mark, Miss Collins?"

Wary of his compliment, Emily eyed him doubtfully, but seeing only admiration, she at last gave a gentle smile. "Thank you, my lord. My uncle was a notable whip and would accept no less in his pupil. As to your cattle, I hope you will not blame the grooms, for 'twas I who ordered the greys and your curricle."

Oliver cocked one dark brow. "I never had a doubt who was responsible."

At that moment young Jamie came dashing up from the gardens, Mrs. Keaton, Sir Ethan and Honoria following behind at a more sedate pace.

"We saw you and Miss Collins racing up the road from yon tower." The boy pointed to the small folly near by the lake which gave one an excellent view of the surrounding countryside.

Hawksworth frowned. "We weren't racing. Miss Collins was just demonstrating her skill with the ribbons."

Sir Ethan grinned, "Aye, I'd say the same, if I had

been the one bringing up the rear, laddie. Me, I'd put my money on the lady in a contest any day."

About to dispute the notion of a race, Hawksworth held his tongue when the sounds of several carriages echoed in the crisp air. Soon, two large traveling coaches and a fourgon loaded with a great many trunks came up the drive, heading for the front of the castle at a moderate pace.

Watching the arrival, all were curious as to the newcomers, but only Delia held a wish as to the identity of the visitor. She hoped that at last Squire Joshua Collins had come to remove his niece from Lord Hawksworth's fatal charms.

Oliver, his mood surprisingly sanguine despite the added burden of new uninvited guests, offered Miss Collins his arm. "Shall we see who has come to pay a visit?"

While Hawksworth had been adjusting to the difficulties of guardianship, his former guests, Mr. Abbot and Mr. Bonham, had returned to Town more than eager to gossip about the house party. With few details or facts, they had titillated Society with the tale of two females and three children, bearing a remarkable resemblance to his lordship, who had arrived at Hawk's Lair bringing the party to an abrupt close with the announcement that the children were his lordship's family.

By the time the story came to the Dowager Lady Hawksworth, it had come to sound as if her grandson was setting up a nursery full of by-blows at the family estate. The lady dismissed the rumors as balderdash, knowing Oliver would never saddle himself with a pack of low-born brats. But when an anxious Lord Halcomb and his daughter arrived within a day, her ladyship knew that action must be taken to ensure that her grandson did not squander his chance at marriage with the wealthy and beautiful Lady Cora.

The marquess, his daughter, Lady Hawksworth and Miss Millet had set out for Hawk's Lair at once. It had been a trying two days' journey, the entourage having to stop every few hours to allow Lady Cora to walk to overcome her carriage sickness. The dowager was thoroughly disgusted by the smell of lavender water which seemed to permeate the marquess's coach, but after all, she wouldn't be the one saddled with the seemingly delicate young beauty.

As the door to the castle was opened by the butler, Lady Hawksworth heard a child's laughter on the afternoon breeze. Before the lady could take a step, two children came dashing round the north tower of the castle. They drew to a halt at the sight of her and the other guests. The dowager was suddenly struck with the notion that she might be wrong about the rumors. She exchanged a questioning glance with Luella Millet, but her companion seemed as puzzled as she.

Oliver too often thumbed his nose at Society. Worry began to tug at the dowager's confidence. Had her grandson gone queer in the attic and brought his base-born offspring to the family seat?

Lady Hawksworth knew quick action was demanded or the scandal would ruin all her plans. She hurried into the Great Hall as her companion, the marquess and his daughter followed.

Nora drew off her pomona-green kid gloves. "Bedows, are there children residing at the castle?"

"Yes, my lady. They are—"

"Luella," her ladyship interrupted, fearing what the

butler was about to say, "accompany Lord Halcomb and Lady Cora to their rooms at once. See to their every comfort."

When the marquess looked as if he might protest, the dowager added, "I am sure you will want to see your daughter safely settled after such an arduous journey as it appears to have been for her. Also you will wish to freshen up before you come to the drawing room to meet my grandson. You can have no doubt that I would prefer a word alone with Hawksworth first. I shall have tea sent up to you."

With a disgruntled look on his lined face, Lord Halcomb took his wilted daughter's other elbow as he and Miss Millet ushered the ailing young lady up the stairs behind a castle footman, the girl's maid trailing behind. Once the party was out of sight, Lady Hawksworth turned to the butler to demand, "I wish to see my grandson in the library. Immediately!"

But before the butler could inform her ladyship that the gentleman was out, the front door opened to admit the earl, escorting two ladies unknown to her, Sir Ethan Russell and the two children her ladyship had seen earlier.

Upon close inspection of the young ones, the dowager's worst fears were realized. The pair looked remarkably like Hawksworth with their dark curls and blue eyes.

Oliver walked up to his grandmother to greet her, but she stood unresponsive as he brushed a kiss on her wrinkled cheek. Seemingly oblivious to the lady's disturbed state, he nonchalantly inquired, "Where is the estimable Miss Millet?"

"Never mind about Luella." She glared at her grandson, then remembering her manners, peered round the

earl. "Good day to you, Sir Ethan." She gave a stiff
nod to the gentleman, then her tone grew haughty and
cold as she swept the women and children with an unfriendly glare. "Who are these people, Hawksworth?"

The earl smiled at the children. "Jamie, Honoria,
come and greet your great-grandmother."

Upon hearing the names of her never-before-seen
great-grandchildren, the fierce look on the dowager's
face changed to one of amazement, then delight. The
young pair stepped obediently forward, but were uncertain about this female who was their father's grandmother. She'd been so angry and sharp, they weren't
certain they wished to meet her.

"My young James and little Honoria, you have come
all the way from India at last." The old woman's grey
eyes grew moist as she extended her arms to the children who hesitantly went to her. The earl quickly explained about the loss of the children's mother during
the birth of the newest Carson, Wesley. Unfortunately,
they still awaited word on the fate of their father. Despite the dark news, the dowager kissed and hugged the
children, telling them not to worry, for they were now
home.

Emily, watching the meeting, was touched by the old
woman's genuine joy at meeting her young descendants.
This greeting was everything that the earl's hadn't been.
Here was the family member who might fulfill all the
children's needs. Emily was pleased, yet she suddenly
felt displaced.

That was, until the old woman's gaze settled on her.
There was a visible coolness in the lady's inquiring eyes.
"Hawksworth, you forget your manners. Introduce your
other guests."

"My lady, may I present Mrs. Delia Keaton and Miss

Emily Collins, who were kind enough to escort the children back from the Indies.

"Ladies, my grandmother, Nora, Dowager Countess of Hawksworth."

The women exchanged polite civilities with the dowager, who offered profound thanks for their bringing the children home. With a wave of her hand, her ladyship then claimed fatigue from her own journey and asked them all to join her in some refreshments. They moved to the Blue Drawing Room, and within minutes Bedows appeared with tea, sandwiches and seed cakes. Lady Hawksworth insisted the children be allowed to remain. Emily and Delia took them to wash their hands, and upon their return there was a very lively tea party.

In no time at all the story of the children's departure from Calcutta due to their father's illness and arrival at the castle had been unfolded in more detail for the countess by first Emily, then Hawksworth. But as the old lady listened to the flow of conversation, she was curious why, after nearly a week, her grandson was still dancing attendance on his wards. And why were the ladies, newly-arrived from Calcutta, still in residence at the castle? Had they no place to be?

It seemed far more likely that Oliver would have hired the proper servants, then come to inform her of the children's arrival. Knowing her grandson, Lady Hawksworth had little doubt it wasn't his wards who were keeping him here.

The dowager soon settled on the reason why her grandson lingered at the castle as she watched the exchange of conversation between Miss Collins and Hawksworth. There was a look of interest in her grandson's eyes as his gaze rested on the young lady that worried Nora deeply.

The countess centered her own attention on this unknown female. The young lady was pretty enough but well past the first blush of youth. She was most certainly not in Oliver's usual style, with her demure ways and unassuming airs. While her gown was well-made, it was neither very stylish nor provocative. She looked very much like any number of country misses one would meet at a local assembly. Not a female who should be intriguing Hawksworth, and yet she was. Suddenly all Nora's plans for her grandson appeared in danger. Was this little nobody from India thinking she might snare herself a titled husband? Not if the countess had anything to say about it—and she would.

As the party broke up, Emily and Delia offered to take the children back to the nursery. With a promise to visit them before dinner and meet her newest great-grandson, the dowager kissed the children farewell. At the same time Sir Ethan excused himself, suspecting that the lady wished a few words of private conversation with her grandson.

Lady Hawksworth watched as the earl's gaze trailed Miss Collins's exit. The countess knew she needed to put a stop to this attraction at once. As the door closed on the lady's back, she said, "Mayhap I should mention that Lord Halcomb and his daughter accompanied me to Hawk's Lair. They are even now resting in their rooms."

There was no show of emotion on her grandson's face at her announcement, but seeing the knuckles whiten on his hand as his fists clenched, Lady Hawksworth knew he was not well pleased. His words confirmed as much.

"What inspired you to drag Halcomb and Lady Cora to Hawk's Lair?"

"The marquess heard rumors not to his liking."

Oliver gave a mirthless laugh. "Rumors! Gad, madam, if he is nervous about a few rumors regarding me, he'd best keep his daughter safe at home in London. My way of life has always been a great topic for the gossips."

Nora leaned back in her chair and gazed intently at the earl. "He is a man of the world, Oliver. He would pay little heed to tales of your numerous dalliances. It was those fools, Abbot and Bonham, dashing about Town gabbling about children taking up residence at the castle—children whose very existence were placed at your door by that pair of coxcombs."

The earl grimaced at the mention of his former house guests. "And now you know the truth. My character is not as black as you and the marquess suspected."

The dowager rose, and her grandson politely followed suit. "Facts which I must go at once and lay out for Halcomb. But Oliver, you cannot continue to dawdle with regard to paying your addresses. Lady Cora is at hand."

Hawksworth opened the door for his grandmother, but there was bitterness in his tone as he remarked, "You will at least allow the lady and me the opportunity to become a little acquainted before I make any irrevocable declarations."

"Of course." So saying, Nora exited the drawing room. As she made her way up the grand staircase, she was worried. Oliver had never been enthusiastic about marrying, and had reluctantly agreed in the first place. But he'd sounded positively morose just now, calling his proposal an irrevocable declaration. What had seemed a simple matter to bring about some two weeks ago now suddenly appeared to be slipping away.

The dowager made her way to the west wing, where

the guests would be quartered. She must have a long talk with the marquess or all their plans might not come to pass. She could only hope that Lady Cora came prepared to win Hawksworth's admiration.

Emily gazed out her window at the fading light. Dressed for dinner in a simple round gown of pink satin with a short train, slashed sleeves and square-cut neckline with silver trim at the bodice and hem, she tugged the white net shawl with silver trim about her shoulders. The announcement that dinner was set back to a more fashionable hour had left her with time on her hands.

There was no denying that she was baffled by her present mood. With the arrival of Lady Hawksworth, all her worries about the children should have flown, but instead she found herself still reluctant to leave the castle. Perhaps it was her feeling that the dowager, while glad to have her great-grandchildren home, was less than delighted about Emily's and Delia's presence. The lady's attitude did not bode well for future visits to Hawk's Lair.

It could only be hoped that once her ladyship got to know them, she would see that they had only the best of intentions. But then, it was the earl who had true authority, and he had unbent considerably since their first night at the castle.

With a sigh, Emily rose after deciding there was no point in worrying. She would make an effort to be pleasant to the countess and hope that the lady would have no objections to Emily and Delia's visits to the children once they were situated in their own home nearby.

Looking at the clock, she realized it was still another

thirty minutes before they would be expected to gather in the Blue Drawing Room. Her gaze fell on the book she'd finished the night before, and she decided to return it to the library as well as make a new selection.

Certain that everyone would be in their rooms dressing, Emily hurried through the empty halls, intent on accomplishing her errand quickly. She arrived at the library and entered, closing the door quietly. The book clutched in her hand, she started towards the stacks, then was forced to duck as great red wings flapped above her head.

To her dismay she realized Juno was out of the new cage, as was Janus, whom she could see perched on the upper library rail peering down at her with interest.

"Oh, Miss Collins, I'm glad ye've come," Sam, the nursery footman, called from near the fireplace. Beside him the children stood, watching their pet birds enjoying a taste of freedom.

"Why are the parrots not in their cage, Jamie?" Emily asked with alarm as she watched Juno land with a broad sweep of wings on the upper rail on the opposite side of the room from her feathered companion.

"Nurse said we might come down and help Sam feed them. I was trying to show him the tricks they can do. Only they won't come back to us when I call them." Jamie scratched his head, puzzled at his pets' strange behavior.

"Whatever are we to do, Miss Collins?" Honoria asked. "Uncle will be ever so angry if we let the birds make a mess in his library as we did his kitchen."

Just then, as if the creature had heard, Juno swooped down low over the great oak desk sending a shower of loose papers flying to the floor. Then, with majestic ease, the red bird sailed upward and landed beside the green parrot again.

Emily knew she must do something quickly. "How do you command them to come to you, Jamie?"

The boy marched to the center of the room, then elevated his left arm. He give a soft whistle, then called first one parrot's name and then the other, but neither responded. Instead, the contrary birds began to preen and squawk as they would have done in the wild. Clearly they were quite content where they were.

Sam moved to stand beside Emily, keeping a wary eye on the lurking great birds, fearful he might be pecked by one of the great beasts. "There be a great butterfly net in the attic, miss. Reckon that might do the trick."

Emily nodded. "Yes, it might. I will remain with the children if you will go and retrieve it, Sam."

The footman went out, but Emily paid little heed, putting her mind to the problem of recapturing the birds. Then a plan formed. "Do you think the parrots will come to me?"

Honoria nodded. "They would come to everyone back home. I don't understand why they are so disobedient tonight."

"Perhaps," Emily said as she went to the desk, "they are still wary of their new home, my dear." She scanned the upper level of the library. The narrow catwalk was safely railed around the entire room and there would be no danger sending the children up the spiral stairs, so she laid out her plan.

Honoria and Jamie understood what was to be done. They hurried up the stairs, then each went in the opposite direction around the catwalk, moving towards the birds slowly. At the same time, Emily climbed up on his lordship's desk and stood in the middle with both her gloved arms extended as Jamie had, whistling for the birds. Her position was scarcely two feet below where the parrots were perched.

The children drew near the parrots, but the wily birds, seeing captors approach, took to wing. They flew about the large room in great swooping dives. Emily remained standing with arms extended and continued to whistle.

At that moment, the door to the library opened and she was vaguely aware of two tall male forms silhouetted in the door. But she was fearful of taking her eyes off the circling and diving parrots. Knowing the danger, she called, "Close the door quickly or the birds will get out." She heard the door click shut.

Just then Juno spread her red wings and swooped down at Emily, but at the last moment, with a soft flutter, the parrot gently lit on the lady's extended left arm. Following suit, Janus circled one last time and glided to Emily's right arm.

"You have done it, Miss Collins. Is she not splendid, Uncle?" Honoria called from the catwalk.

Emily's gaze went immediately to the earl, looking handsome in his evening black. Her heart fluttered much like the birds' great wings when the gentleman smiled at her, saying, "So she is, my dear niece."

Embarrassed by the trembling which seemed to come unbidden to her knees, Emily drew her gaze to the second gentleman. He was a stranger, and from the look on his lined face, not one happy to be at Hawk's Lair. Tall and greying, with gaunt features, the gentleman was dressed in a black evening coat and white waistcoat, but somehow looked less splendid than the earl despite the similarity in their attire.

As the birds' talons dug into the white gloves which

protected her arms, Emily suddenly realized she didn't
know what to do now that she had them. "I am not
sure how splendid I am, for I cannot get down to put
these two back where they belong."

The earl stepped forward. "Jamie, Honoria, come
down slowly. I feel certain the birds will allow you to
put them back, since they have known you the longest."

The children came down the stairs and slowly made
their way to where Miss Collins stood like a statue,
praying the parrots didn't take flight again.

The earl positioned them on either side of the desk.
"Bend down, Miss Collins and the children will each
take one of your feathered friends."

Jamie and Honoria, long familiar with their pets, each
extended an arm and the parrots stepped onto the new
perches without the least fanfare. The children moved
them to the cage and quickly closed the door once the
birds were safely behind the bars.

The earl turned and grinned at Emily. "I won't ask
how this all came to be. It is what I have come to
expect in my new life as guardian. May I assist you
down, Miss Collins?"

Before Emily could say a word, the gentleman put
his hands about her waist and lifted her to the floor as
if she were as light as a dried leaf. Briefly his hands
lingered, feeling warm through her gown as he gazed
into her eyes and asked, "Are you unharmed? The birds
didn't scratch your arms?"

It took her a moment to gather her thoughts. As his
hands dropped away, she took a step back and then
made a great show of smoothing her gloves back into
place. "Not a bit, my lord. I assure you, I am fine."

The earl's gaze lingered on her face for a moment
longer before he seemed to come to his senses. "Then

allow me to present you to the Marquess of Halcomb. My lord, Miss Emily Collins."

The scowl on the older gentleman's face was anything but welcoming. Despite his grim look, the marquess said all that was polite, even inquiring about her journey from Calcutta.

After several minutes of polite yet stilted conversation, Hawksworth said, " 'Tis almost time to join the others. Would you be so kind as to return these imps to Nurse, Miss Collins, or shall I?"

Feeling uncomfortable under the marquess's unwelcome stare, Emily assured the earl that she would be delighted to see the children safely to the nursery.

With a hug for their uncle and a polite bow to the new guest, the children exited the room, Emily following. In that moment before the library door closed behind her, Emily heard the marquess's angry tones. "I am displeased with your conduct, Hawksworth. That woman—"

What else the gentleman said was lost as the oak portal clicked shut, but Emily was curious who this marquess was and what he had to do with the earl. She led the children up the stairs, but her mind was full of the strange undertones now present at the castle. Was she in some way to blame?

Whatever was the matter with her? She wondered. First his grandmother had seemed to take her in dislike, and now, so it would seem, had the marquess as well. Then that dark thought was lost as she remembered the exciting feel of the earl's hands at her waist and the way the blood had rushed in her ears. She reminded herself that the gentleman was an accomplished rake. Doubtless the moment had affected him little.

Perhaps it was just as well that others had come. It

would keep her from being too much alone in his lord-ship's company and that might be the safest thing for her own well-being.

"I am displeased with your conduct, Hawksworth. That woman should be on her way to wherever it is she resides. It is an insult to my daughter that you—"

"My lord"—the earl's back stiffened at the rebuke, his face becoming a frigid mask—"I think you forget that whatever plans you and my grandmother have laid are just that—yours. I am fully prepared to admire your daughter and give my grandmother's wishes due con-sideration. Beyond that I make no promises. My first consideration at this time must be my wards and seeing them comfortably settled in their new home."

Oliver felt a brief twinge of guilt to be using the children to dodge his grandmother's plans, but in truth, he knew he had come to care about their welfare.

The marquess's face grew red. "Do you have any—"

At that moment the library door opened and Sam stepped in, butterfly net in hand. "Sorry, my lord, didn't know you was in here. Just came to—" Seeing the birds back in their cage, he bowed. "Miss Collins got them creatures back where they belong. She's a right 'un."

Hawksworth, not wishing a prolonged argument with his guest, moved to the doorway. "Sam, see that my papers are picked up and put back on my desk." Look-ing back at the marquess, the earl added, "I think we have said all we need to for now. Shall we go to the drawing room and await the ladies, my lord?"

A glowering marquess marched past his host out of the library. "Think I'd best see how my daughter's health is after the journey here."

Halcomb wasn't happy with the earl's declaration, but he was not prepared to give up. Cora had her heart set on being a countess and that was what she would be. He knew that with a little luck and the dowager's help, they would still see an engagement before they departed Hawk's Lair.

Eight

Lady Cora Lane was a Diamond of the First Water. It had been an acknowledged fact in the *ton* these five years. Guinea-gold curls framed a heart-shaped face of porcelain-white skin. Her aqua-blue eyes were large, with long brown lashes and delicately arched brows, her ruby lips full above a tilt-tipped nose. There were few who did not own that the marquess's daughter would have rivaled the goddesses of legend. Unfortunately, upon closer acquaintance, there were few whose opinion of the lady could be found to be as high as her own.

She'd arrived in London at the tender age of eighteen with the advantages of birth, beauty and fortune. Alas for her marital hopes, her sharp tongue and arrogance soon drove all but the most desperate fortune hunters to seek out the lesser lights of the Season.

Lady Cora had gone home from that first Season unbetrothed, but convinced it was only because of the paltry number of eligible candidates. Yet the results of successive Seasons had ultimately been the same.

Having reached the advanced age of three-and-twenty unwed, the lady's desperation had added a shrewishness to her manner. Her father had begun to fear that his beautiful daughter would be left on the shelf, which meant she would be under his roof, wreaking havoc on his peace, for a lifetime. Then salvation had come in the form of the Dowager Countess of Hawksworth, who'd hinted of arranging a marriage of convenience with her raffish grandson.

Lady Cora knew of the earl's unsavory reputation, but his wealth and impeccable lineage made him a perfect husband in her opinion. In truth, she was completely content with the notion that he would keep a mistress and not bother her, so she'd made up her mind that the thing she wanted most was to be Countess of Hawksworth.

Presently the lady was lounging on a day bed in her elegantly appointed room in the west wing, attempting to recover from the rigors of the journey south. Her maid, having just returned from below stairs with tea and toast, was unpacking the numerous trunks and imparting all the gossip she'd gleaned from the castle servants about his lordship.

Lady Cora was now aware that Hawk's Lair was a bit topsy-turvy because of the arrival of several children and females from India, some relations of the earl. Certain that these people had nothing to do with her, she put the matter from her mind.

A sharp knock caused Maggie to fall silent as Lady Cora signaled her to the door. Lord Halcomb entered his daughter's room and ordered the maid gone in a gruff voice.

Lady Cora sat up, taking note that her father's face looked a thundercloud. "Whatever is the matter, Papa?"

"Why are you not dressed, child?"

"There is no rush. Besides, I thought to make an entrance in my new blue sarcenet gown with the white beading. The cut of the dress complements my—"

"Don't be talking about your fripperies, girl. I just spoke with Hawksworth, and matters are not as settled as the dowager would have us believe."

Lady Cora's cheeks blanched white. "What do you mean? I am to be the countess. You said so. I demand you keep your promise."

Lord Halcomb eyed his daughter warily. The one thing he didn't want was a tantrum for all to hear. "And so I shall, my little dove, if I have anything to say about the matter. But remember, you have never formally met the earl, nor he you. He seems to feel there should be a period of acquaintance before anything definite is decided. Problem is that he's just acquired his brother's children and seems much involved in his role as guardian."

"Children!" Lady Cora said the word as if she spoke of some vile affliction. "You know how I dislike them, Papa. The noise, the dirt, and their flying about from one mischief to another. Why, I had to cut Lady Albina from my acquaintance due to her forever wishing to display those dreadful boys every time one paid a visit. I simply cannot abide children."

In truth, it had been the baroness who'd ceased to invite Lady Cora after the young lady had remarked on the children looking rather like monkeys with all that dark hair and forever climbing about in the trees outside the drawing room.

Halcomb wagged his finger at his daughter. "You will not only abide these children, my dear, you will convince the earl they are the dearest things in nature, if you take my advice. I would never have thought it, but London's most notorious rake seems to actually like the little monsters."

"But, Papa, I cannot!" The lady rose from the daybed, a hint of tears filling her lovely eyes.

The marquess was not the least bit swayed, for he'd seen such a display over as simple a matter as his refusal to purchase a new fan. He took her by the shoulders and gave her a gentle shake. "You must be guided by me, child. None of your high-in-the-instep manners or ill-advised tantrums here. You must be all politeness to the earl and his guests."

A look of horror crossed Lady Cora's beautiful face. "But Papa, Maggie says there are several hurly-burly females presently staying at the castle just returned from India without so much as a gentleman to escort them. Not to mention a barbaric Scotsman. You cannot think I should unbend myself to take notice of such inferior sorts."

"Do you wish to be a countess?"

She gave a vigorous nod of her head, her blond curls bouncing.

"Then you will condescend to make yourself agreeable to Hawksworth's guests and his wards. There will be time enough after the wedding to have things to your own liking. Now get dressed at once. There is no time to waste." With that the marquess left the room.

Oliver lifted the cut-crystal top off the decanter and poured out a good measure of brandy. Taking his glass, he moved to the window of the drawing room to stare out at the darkness, which seemed to perfectly reflect his present mood. What had he been thinking to agree to his grandmother's suggestion of a marriage to a female he'd never been introduced to? If the surly Lord

Halcomb was any indication, he was likely to take a dislike to Lady Cora on sight.

He swirled the amber liquid, knowing that due to the dowager's interference, he must at least give the lady a fair chance. While he'd made no declarations, his promise to his grandfather still hung over him like an executioner's sword. No doubt Lady Cora was as suitable as any female and had the advantage of birth and fortune, which seemed so important to his grandmother.

Then his thoughts turned to another female. He remembered the feel of Miss Collins's slender waist as he'd lifted her from his desk and his lusty response. There had been such a rush of desire that he'd had to resist the urge to pull her to him and kiss her lovely mouth.

Abruptly he put down his brandy. He'd promised his grandmother to give the idea of marrying Lady Cora a proper chance. He had no business having thoughts about Miss Collins when his mind should rightly be turned to the matter of his prospective fiancée.

To the earl's relief, the door to the drawing room opened, and Sir Ethan stepped into the room. The men fell into idle conversation until the next guests arrived. As the marquess and his daughter entered the room, Oliver felt the muscles in his stomach tighten, although he wasn't certain why.

As the introductions were made, he took his first good look at the woman his grandmother had deemed a suitable match. There could be no denying that she was a beauty. Her blond curls were drawn away from her lovely face and decorated with two small blue plumes complementing her aqua eyes, which surveyed him frankly. She would certainly be a woman that a man would be proud to have on his arm. Then the memory of the violent quarrels between his father and stepmother flooded his mind, and Oliver knew there was much more to marriage than social appearances.

"My lord," Lady Cora said, offering her hand as she smiled up at him engagingly. "I hope you will forgive my positively hagged appearance, but I fear the journey from London rather shattered my nerves."

Oliver was certain she could have little doubt about the excellence of her looks and was forced to suppress a frown as he wondered if she was the kind of female always fishing for compliments.

"If you were any more lovely this evening, Lady Cora, the very angels in heaven would weep." Oliver kissed the proffered hand, but found that he said the words mechanically, without the least attraction to this veritable goddess.

The lady twittered girlishly. "I do believe all I have heard of you, sir, is quite true."

"Heard?" Oliver asked warily.

"That you are charming as well as handsome, my lord."

Sir Ethan, well aware of the earl's dislike of toadying, remarked, "Bless me, lass, if that's all you've heard of my friend, he can count himself lucky."

Oliver frowned a warning at the baronet, then ushered the marquess and his daughter to a sofa near the fireplace. They were soon joined by Lady Hawksworth, dressed regally in dark red, then Mrs. Keaton and Miss Collins, both lovely in varying shades of pink.

Lady Cora, after condescending to offer two fingers of her hand for the ladies to shake at being introduced, soon dominated the conversation. She paid scant heed to anyone but his lordship, announcing that she found everything at the castle to her liking. Then she went on to inform them that it was only matched by the splendor of her father's manor in Surrey.

During the lady's rambling discourse, the marquess closely watched Hawksworth's reaction to both his daughter and Miss Collins. He liked neither look. For Cora there was mere polite interest, but for Miss Collins there were intimate smiles.

Oblivious to all but herself, Lady Cora began to discuss the latest *on-dits* in Society, but Lord Halcomb stepped in to change the direction of the conversation. He determined to drop a flea in his daughter's ear about letting her tongue run on wheels.

"What are your plans for your wards, my lord?" The marquess gave the countess a conspiratory smile, knowing from their earlier conversation that the lady was still dedicated to the proposed match.

"Plans?" Oliver frowned at Halcomb.

"Are they to remain at the castle, to be sent to a proper school or do you intend to bring them to London?"

Very aware of Miss Collins's intent gaze upon him, the earl replied, "I believe they have had enough upheaval in their lives this year. For the present they will remain here. I intend, with Miss Collins's help, to interview several applicants for the position of governess."

"Miss Collins!" The voices of Lord Halcomb, Lady Cora and Lady Hawksworth echoed together.

Emily felt her cheeks warm at the hostile looks turned in her direction. She suddenly wished she were anyplace but in his lordship's drawing room. Why ever did they all dislike her so?

Coming to the lady's defense, the earl said, "Both Miss Collins and Mrs. Keaton have been generous with their time, helping me settle the children in the castle, assisting with new wardrobes for the cold weather and caring for the children while I find proper servants. Guardianship of very young ones is not a matter most bachelors handle easily."

At that moment Bedows arrived to announce dinner. The party moved to the huge dining room, where painted cherubs looked down upon the gathering. Emily was glad they were mere wood and paint, for she felt certain that otherwise they too would be hurling arrows at her.

She found herself seated between the scowling marquess and the unfriendly dowager. She couldn't have been less happy. It was a struggle to down the surprisingly elaborate fare of the new cook.

Her thoughts went to the possibility of leaving Hawk's Lair. After all, the countess was here to advise the earl, and clearly the lady seemed to think Emily was pushing herself forward in an improper manner. But when the notion of leaving left her feeling unhappy, she attributed it to the fact she would miss the children. It had nothing to do with the earl.

Just then she glanced down the table to see Sir Ethan and Delia conversing with great pleasure. Emily wondered if she would spoil her companion's chance for a possible match with the delightful baronet if they left the castle. Remembering what a dreadful first marriage Delia had suffered, Emily didn't want her friend to miss an opportunity to capture the heart of such a kind man as Sir Ethan. Despite Lady Hawksworth's hostility, Emily decided they would stay a while longer.

Emily was startled from her musings when the countess addressed her.

"Have you been enjoying your stay at Hawk's Lair,

Miss Collins?" The dowager's grey eyes narrowed as she awaited Emily's answer.

"It has been a bit hectic, my lady, getting the children settled. But yes, it has been enjoyable to be home in England."

"Then I shall make certain Hawksworth invites you for the wedding."

Emily's hand trembled as she laid down her fork. "There is to be a wedding?"

A satisfied smile tipped the countess's lined mouth as she looked down the table at the marquess's daughter. "Did you not know? My grandson is soon to become affianced to Lady Cora. That is why we have come. Finding my great-grandchildren at the castle merely adds to my joy on this momentous occasion."

Lady Hawksworth, glancing back at Miss Collins, watched a dull glaze settled in the young lady's brown eyes even as she said all the proper things. One might almost feel sorry for the girl—but not one who had made plans for her grandson that did not include a marriage to a veritable nobody.

The countess would have been greatly surprised if she'd been privy to the thoughts in Miss Collins's head. Her initial disappointment was great at hearing the news of impending nuptials. But Emily determinedly put thoughts of the earl aside. While he was a handsome man, there had been little between them except matters pertaining to the children, and after all, he was a rake. That was something she reminded herself of every time she found his gaze resting upon her with interest.

She decided that her primary concern must be for the children and what role Lady Cora would play in their lives. In effect, the lady would be the children's new mother. Emily peered down the table at the young woman. There was no denying that she was beautiful, a fact that Lady Cora seemed well aware of, but was there compassion and caring beneath that seemingly vain exterior?

Would she be one of those ladies who spent all her time in London in the social whirl? Would Lady Cora undo all that had been accomplished with the earl's growing attachment to his wards? The very thought made Emily's blood stir in anger.

She knew it was none of her concern, yet her love for the children would not let her ignore their fate. Was Lady Cora prepared for such a responsibility as marrying the earl would now entail? It was the height of impertinence on Emily's part to be asking such a question, even of herself. Still, it wasn't the first time she'd involved herself in Lord Hawksworth's affairs since her arrival at the castle.

In truth, Emily wondered if she might be making a rash assumption about the young lady. She hardly knew Lady Cora. Nevertheless, Emily was determine to stay and see for herself what kind of female the earl had chosen to fill such a place in his wards' lives.

The evening seemed interminable to Oliver. His gaze drifted to Sir Ethan, Mrs. Keaton and Miss Collins on the far side of the Blue Drawing Room examining a book about the Indies the baronet had found in the library. That was where Oliver longed to be, but instead manners forced him to politely remain at his grandmother's side.

Where had all his pleasure gone with his quiet evenings at Hawk's Lair? It seemed to have disappeared with the arrival of his grandmother, the marquess and

Lady Cora. The previously interesting conversation with the ladies from Calcutta regarding books, art and the exotic land from which they'd returned had been replaced with Lady Cora's and the dowager's chatter about fashion, scandals and common acquaintances, as well as the marquess's broad hints about wanting to discuss marriage, which Oliver chose to ignore.

He wanted to invite the others to join his group, but he hadn't been blind to Lady Cora's or his grandmother's cool treatment of both Miss Collins and Mrs. Keaton. He knew Sir Ethan's bringing the book had been his way to protect the ladies from the gentle snubs of the new guests.

This night was so much like every dull evening he'd spent upon first arriving in Town that he suddenly remembered what had made him scorn the fashionable pursuits and go his own way. As he gazed at the beautiful Lady Cora, he wondered if he were looking at the vision of his future boring life.

At long last Bedows arrived with the tea tray, and the earl knew the ordeal was almost over. To his surprise, his grandmother asked if the children were still awake. Bedows informed the lady that the older children were, but they were dressed for bed.

Looking at the marquess, the dowager announced, "Oh, we are almost all family here. Have the dears come down to say good night."

Lady Cora, tired from her evening of being charming, wanted to scream and stamp her feet at having to pretend to like the earl's wards, but seeing the look on her father's face, she said, "I am looking forward to meeting your young relatives, my lord."

Oliver looked at the lady with some surprise. He would not have expected her to be much interested in his wards, for he himself hadn't been at first. Perhaps females were quite different about such matters. "They are remarkable in the way they have handled all their hardships, Lady Cora."

Minutes later, Jamie and Honoria, their night-clothes covered by new brocade dressing gowns, bounded into the room. They went immediately to their great-grandmother and kissed her rouged cheek. The dowager proudly introduced her young relatives to Lord Halcomb and Lady Cora.

The children acquitted themselves respectably with a bow and a curtsey, but as Honoria rose from her wobbly dip, she froze and stared at Lady Cora with a puzzled expression on her face.

As the silence grew, Lady Cora became uncomfortable. "Whatever is the matter? Why do you stare at me like a moonling, girl?"

"You have plumes in your hair."

Lady Cora preened and patted the curls that held the small blue feathers. "Yes, 'tis the fashion." Then, thinking to impress his lordship, she pulled one small plume free and extended it to the little girl.

Honoria shook her head, but eyed the feather longingly. "Thank you kindly, but I must not take it. Ladies of Quality do not wear such. They are quite vulgar, you know."

Sir Ethan gave a laugh that he managed to change to a cough as the earl frowned at his niece.

With an angry twitter, the marquess's daughter snapped, "Where did you hear such a ridiculous thing?"

Oliver knew he must take action. "Honoria, you will apologize at once. Of course genteel ladies wear feathers."

Emily and Delia exchanged a look. How could they

explain about the actresses and the great dyed plumes without betraying the earl before his soon-to-be fiancée? But neither did Emily want the child to be censured for their mistake. "I fear Delia and I are to blame for Honoria's misconception. She witnessed a lady with an excess of bright red plumes on a bonnet quite recently. We but explained that a lady did not dress in such a manner. I fear she thought we meant all feathers." She looked at Hawksworth pointedly to remind him of a particular vulgarly ornate hat.

Oliver knew in an instant where his niece had seen such a bonnet. Colette Devereau's had been such. Seeing the angry flush on Lady Cora's face because of the child's unintentional insult, he was determined to calm the waters.

"A reasonable mistake for a child to make. Honoria, you may take this feather, for it is just the type the fashionable ladies wear. Thank Lady Cora."

The child eagerly took the feather and thanked the lady, but Emily feared that the damage had been done. Lady Cora behaved as if the incident was of no importance and continued to engage the earl in conversation, but Emily felt certain she detected a hint of malice in the aqua eyes each time they came to rest on the little girl.

As the hour grew long, Emily noted the children begin to yawn. Still the dowager seemed more interested in the conversation of her grandson and his future fiancée.

Rising, Emily said, " 'Tis becoming quite late. Shall I return the children to the nursery, Lady Hawksworth?"

"That won't be necessary, Miss Collins. I think you have done quite enough with the children for now." Lady Hawksworth's tone was frigid as she rose. "Come, my dears, Lady Cora and I shall see you safely back to your beds."

Lady Cora was less than pleased but managed to suppress her grimace before his lordship saw her true feeling. With a smirk at Emily, the young lady followed the dowager and the children from the room. Lord Halcomb rose and bade good night to all, then followed his daughter.

Emily's cheeks warmed at the dowager's pointed snub, and she gazed at the carpet mutely. She tried to tell herself that the dowager had a right to be angry with them over Honoria's faux pas, but she suspected there was more to the lady's attitude than Emily's influence on the children.

Aware that someone had moved to her side, Emily looked up into the smiling eyes of the earl. "Don't look so glum, Miss Collins. There was no serious harm done by Honoria, and I am sure that Lady Cora understood."

"I hope you are right, sir. But your grandmother seems much offended." Suddenly Emily felt like an intruder in the Carson family. "I think, my lord, it is perhaps time that Delia and I continued on our journey."

Oliver knew he didn't want her to leave. He was furious with his grandmother's conduct. In her zeal to promote Lady Cora, she had allowed herself to appear rude to Miss Collins, whom he knew they owed a great debt—or at least that was what his mind kept telling him. Well, he wouldn't allow her to leave under a cloud.

"You cannot abandon me with the task of interviewing all those governesses alone. Only think what terrors their hearts will experience to be in such notorious company as mine. Besides, left to my own devices, I am certain I shall hire the wrong one."

Emily realized at once that his lordship was trying to

make up for his grandmother's insult, and her heart warmed. She knew she must not read too much into his attempt to cover his relative's rudeness, but still she found herself pleased that he wanted her to stay.

"I don't think you need worry about hiring the wrong governess unless you advertised at the local opera house." After the earl chuckled, Emily added, "But I shall not abandon you and the children, my lord."

With that, Emily and Delia said their good nights and made their way upstairs. As the maid helped her undress, Emily knew that Lady Hawksworth would not be well pleased with her decision to stay longer. Clearly the lady saw her as a threat to the betrothal of Lady Cora and his lordship, but Emily couldn't imagine why. She and the earl had spent more time quarreling than anything else. All the same, Emily thought it best if she kept her distance from the gentleman. With a deep sigh, she climbed into bed and tried to get some sleep.

In the drawing room, the gentlemen settled before the fire with glasses of brandy. Sir Ethan was conscious of his friend's dark mood as they sat together in silence. He was well aware of Oliver's reluctance to marry and could even sympathize, having had such a bad time of it himself when he'd taken the plunge years ago. But it was plain to see the countess was here to advance Lady Cora as the future Countess of Hawksworth.

At last, hoping to lighten his friend's mood, the baronet asked, "Did I hear Miss Collins say that she and Delia are leaving?"

"Delia, is it?" Oliver managed a half smile for his friend despite his bedeviled mood.

The baronet returned the smile. "Only between us,

for the lass hasn't given me permission to take such a liberty. Not yet, that is."

"I do believe it is midsummer madness for you and 'tis but March. Shall I be wishing you happy soon?" The earl's eye held a hint of wistfulness as he watched his friend. Why could he not have been bewitched by Lady Cora?

Then the thought came unbidden that he *was* bewitched, but by someone else. He pushed such an odd idea away and tried to concentrate on what his friend was saying.

"You are become like a matchmaking old woman, Hawksworth. While I find the lady amusing, I am not ready to take the leap into parson's mousetrap. I do believe you are the one expected to do that—and soon."

Oliver ran his fingers through his hair, returning his gaze to the flames. "I would as soon leap off one of the turrets at the castle as marry Lady Cora Lane. The pain would be short and sweet compared to a lifetime of insipid conversation and boring nights."

The baronet looked around the room in a broad gesture. "Don't see anyone here holding a gun to your head, laddie. You promised your grandfather to marry. Nothing says it has to be some rich, beautiful . . ." Sir Ethan seemed to struggle a moment with the description, then seemed to give up and added, "silly, caper-witted goosecap selected by your grandmother."

"I know," Oliver said, then he came to a decision and rose. "And so I shall tell her at once. Sleep well, my friend."

He made his way up to the lady's room, his irate mood growing with each step. It wasn't just that the countess was demanding he declare himself to a woman whom he found intolerable, but that she was also being rude to his other guests in her quest to bring about the match.

On being bidden to enter after his knock, the earl found his grandmother sitting up in bed with a book before her.

"What brings you to me so late, Oliver? Have you good news about Lady Cora?"

"Madam, you will cease this matchmaking at once. I appreciate the efforts you have gone to in order to find me a proper wife, but can you honestly say that you like the marquess's daughter?"

Nora looked down at her covers, tugging at them guiltily with her frail fingers. "I find her little different from the other young ladies of the *ton*."

"Exactly so. She is empty-headed, vain and I would suspect ill-tempered when thwarted. Is this the woman you would choose to help me care for and manage your great-grandchildren?" Oliver came and stood beside the bed as he made his argument. He thought the lady looked surprisingly old without any of the feminine artifices to enhance her. He could see the veins beneath her white and lined skin.

Despite appearances, the countess was no frail thing who would give in during a fight. Her grey eyes stared at him unflinchingly. "So you now will fail to honour your promise to wed because of a few minor flaws in Lady Cora?"

"Grandmother, I am perfectly capable of finding a bride on my own. A bride I won't wish to strangle the very first night."

The dowager's brows drew together. "Oliver, you cannot marry just any female. Your reputation is such that you must find a lady whose character is beyond reproach."

Oliver turned and walked to the door, pausing before he departed. "And so I shall, but you must cease your matchmaking with Lady Cora. She and her father are welcome to stay as long as they like, but I shall not make her an offer."

"You will whistle down a fortune if you let such a lady slip through your fingers. Don't let your fascination with that nobody from India ruin your chances for an excellent alliance."

"Miss Collins has nothing to do with my feeling about Lady Cora." Oliver spoke with such vehemence that he startled even himself. Then, hoping to distract his grandmother from his reaction, he added, "And while we are on the subject, you will kindly refrain from your rude conduct to both Miss Collins and Mrs. Keaton. Don't forget that without their kindness, your grandchildren might still be in India with only servants to care for them if my brother is dead. I believe you owe them an apology."

At that Nora fell silent. Had she let her obsession with bringing about a match between the marquess's daughter and her grandson blind her to Miss Collins's and Mrs. Keaton's goodness? Perhaps. She would make an effort to be kinder. Still, she wasn't prepared to accept that Oliver might miss the opportunity for such a splendid match with Lady Cora.

"I shall mend my ways, but you must promise me you will make no decision about Lady Cora until you know the young lady better."

Seeing the hopeful look in his grandmother's eyes, Oliver didn't have the heart to dash all her dreams. "Whatever I do, I shall take my time. You can be certain that I shall certainly be a proper host and entertain all my guests to the best of my ability."

With that the countess had to be content. Her grandson wished her a good night and left.

Nora was still convinced that Oliver would eventually fall prey to Lady Cora's beauty, if the girl would just mind her tongue. She would have a word with the marquess in the morning. The lady blew out the candles and settled down to sleep, still hopeful that her plans might come to pass.

Nine

A steady spring rain forced the residents of Hawk's Lair to stay captive indoors the following day. Emily, keeping with her resolution, decided she would escape any unnecessary encounters with the earl. After breakfast, during which the countess had been surprisingly civil, Emily returned upstairs to her sitting room determined to while away the time reading. She encouraged her companion to join the others downstairs, hopeful that the lady would be able to spend the morning in company with Sir Ethan.

But scarcely an hour later, Delia returned with Honoria and Jamie in tow. As the children moved to the window to argue about how long the downpour would last, Delia came to sit near Emily. In a low whisper, Delia said, "Lady Cora demanded that I remove the children from the drawing room. They were giving her the headache."

"And Lord Hawksworth agreed to them being sent away?" Emily's tone held an angry edge as she wondered if the lady's influence on his lordship was so strong.

"Oh, he and Sir Ethan were called to the stable after breakfast to confer with Bates about a sick horse. Why did you not tell me that Lady Cora was to become the children's aunt?"

Emily tugged at the fringe on her blue cashmere shawl. "Did Lord Hawksworth tell you that?"

" 'Twas the countess who informed me that was the reason they came to the castle. She proclaims it is her fondest wish that one day soon the lady would be sharing responsibility for the children with their uncle. I tell you, my dear, it was all I could do to keep from telling her ladyship that Lady Cora hadn't a maternal bone in her body. Oh, she is all sweetness and condescension to the children when the earl and her ladyship are present, but she did little to hide her dislike of Honoria and Jamie once he and the countess were gone."

The news did not surprise Emily. "Do you think we should do something to reveal her deception to them?"

Delia eyed her employer fearfully. The last thing she wanted was for Emily to be more involved in the earl's affairs. "Heavens, no. I feel certain that the earl will see through her ploy, even if the countess does not. Time will do the trick. I think the more the lady must deal with the children, the more difficult it will be for her to mask her true feelings." Still, Delia couldn't bear thinking about the children being under the thumb of the selfish Lady Cora.

"But once Lord Hawksworth has declared himself, he cannot in all honor draw back. Surely we should—"

"Miss Collins, Mrs. Keaton?" Honoria came dashing up to the ladies, interrupting their whispered conversation. "Can we not play a game?"

The suggestion had merit for Delia, since she hoped to distract Emily from concocting some plan to discredit Lady Cora. "An excellent notion, my dear. What say you, Emily?"

Seeing the expectant look on both the children's faces, Emily smiled. "Just the thing to enliven a rainy day. What do you suggest?"

It was soon settled that they would play a game of hide and seek in the west wing, since only they occupied the floor at the moment. They idled away much of the morning with the simple entertainment, but at nuncheon the children returned to the nursery and the ladies went downstairs to join the others.

Emily noted that the earl was polite to all but looked bored. Lady Cora and the countess dominated the conversation, and Hawksworth rarely commented save when Sir Ethan made some remark.

Not that Emily could blame him, for both she and Delia knew little of the doings of Society and in truth found much of the gossip the ladies discussed a dead bore. As the meal progressed, she looked up to find the earl's steady blue gaze upon her. Her heart began to race when his sensuous mouth tipped up into a smile she felt certain was meant for her. Then his grandmother, ever vigilant of his straying attention, asked him some inane question which required an answer, and the intimate moment was gone.

As the conversation ebbed and flowed about her, Emily was puzzled by the earl's polite but distant treatment of Lady Cora. It seemed to Emily that whatever Lady Hawksworth's plans, the earl was little inclined to pursue a betrothal. That thought left her in a lighthearted mood.

After the meal, there was little change in the day's routine dullness. Lady Hawksworth invited Lady Cora to her room for a coze when the gentlemen decided to engage in a game of billiards. Emily and Delia returned to their own sitting room to handle personal tasks, knowing the children would be resting.

Delia attempted to discuss either pursuing the purchase of a house in Somersetshire or setting a time to remove from Hawk's Lair to London, but Emily only put her off, saying she was too concerned about the children to leave just yet. When Emily walked to the window to stand in thought, Delia at last gave up and picked up her sewing. After several moments, Emily remarked that the sun was coming out from behind the diminishing clouds. She prophesied that the morrow would be sunny, and they fell into a brief discussion of the weather. But after a time they became quiet, each with her own thoughts.

Without warning, Emily remarked, "I think you are correct about Lady Cora."

Delia, startled from her thoughts about a handsome Scotsman, looked up from her stitchery. "What do you mean?"

Emily smiled, but there was a speculative look in her amber eyes. "The lady needs to spend more time with the children."

"To be sure, but how do you intend to make that happen? As soon as his lordship goes about his business, she will make some excuse to be rid of them."

"Then we must make certain that Lord Hawksworth is included in our plans. What say you to a picnic on the morrow?"

Delia put aside her sewing and came to Emily. "You cannot be taking such domestic matters into your hands. The countess will take exception to your pushing yourself forward in such an unbecoming manner."

Emily knew her companion was correct. "There must be some way to suggest such an outing without being impolite." She grew quiet for a moment, then a smile lit her face. "Do you think Sir Ethan would make such a suggestion to the earl? I am certain he would do it for you."

Delia blushed, but shyly said, "I know he does not like the lady. There is only one way to know. I shall ask him at dinner."

When the appointed time to dine arrived, Emily was quite anxious to join the others. She watched as Delia drew the baronet aside before the gong sounded for dinner. But to her disappointment, the gentleman frowned and seemed to have little to say to Mrs. Keaton. At last the pair rejoined the group, but neither Delia nor Sir Ethan gave any indication as to the outcome of their discussion.

The evening moved slowly, much like the night before, only this night Emily avoided any private conversation with the earl and made a concerted effort to be pleasant to the countess, who in her turn was very sociable. The children again came to the drawing room when the tea tray was brought.

Emily watched Lady Cora closely. After fawning over Honoria and Jamie on their arrival, she pasted a patently false smile on her face and seemed to physically recoil from them as they sat beside her. The lady wanted no part of the responsibility of caring for children. No doubt she would see them all enrolled in remote schools the first chance she got.

With a determined sigh, Emily made up her mind to broach the subject of a picnic with the earl before she retired, no matter the impropriety. But to her delight, Sir Ethan joined in the plan.

"I believe tomorrow is promising to be a delightful day, Hawksworth. Do you think Cook could make arrangements for a picnic on the estate on such short notice?"

Honoria, hearing of a picnic, jumped up from her position beside the dowager and rushed to take her uncle's hand. She tugged it gently, saying, "Oh, Uncle, please say that we may go as well. There is nothing Jamie and I like better than to eat out of doors."

Oliver's gaze moved to Emily. "We must make certain that our guests would enjoy such an outing."

In an unseemly rush, Emily said, "My lord, I know that Delia and I should greatly relish a chance to enjoy the English countryside once more."

Jamie threw his arm around the neck of the countess. "Will you come too, Great-grandmama?"

Lady Hawksworth smiled indulgently at the boy. "Good heavens, child, I am much too old to be dining on the ground, but I shall not spoil your fun. You may all have your picnic. Luella and I shall remain indoors. I have several friends I wish to write to and announce the arrival of my delightful great-grandchildren." With that she tweaked Jamie's nose.

The marquess, seeing the mutinous look on his daughter's face, quickly spoke before she could refuse. "I shall keep the ladies company here, but I am certain that my daughter would enjoy whatever outing is decided upon."

Lady Cora gave a wan smile. "To be sure, I should enjoy dining alfresco. Such fun."

Oliver stared at the lady briefly. He was not in the least fooled by her false pronouncement. But he knew for certain that such an outing would be a welcome relief from the dull doings into which the castle had fallen. "Then I shall make the arrangements. Shall we set the time for two tomorrow afternoon?"

Everyone who was going agreed. Emily knew she was looking forward to an afternoon spent with the earl and away from the countess's watchful eyes. If Lady Cora's true self was revealed in the course of the outing, all the better.

The following morning the spring air held only a slight chill, and the sunny afternoon was perfect for the proposed outing. The servants worked busily setting up a table loaded with a variety of food and drink near the ornamental lake. Several large blankets were spread upon the ground with shade umbrellas positioned so that the ladies might dine in comfort.

Emily, Delia and the two eldest children—the countess had deemed Wesley too young—as well as the excited Kali, arrived to find Lord Hawksworth and Sir Ethan standing beside Lady Cora, who'd settled upon a blanket near the water's edge. The lady looked a picture in a white muslin gown with a sheer overdress of white embroidered flowers. A straw bonnet with pink ribbons framed her beautiful face.

Emily gave the lady but a cursory glance, for her gaze was drawn to his lordship, who stood smiling as he watched their approach. A light breeze ruffled his raven-black hair, giving him a boyish charm, yet his blue eyes held a sensuous light that made Emily's heart beat faster. Embarrassed at where her thoughts wandered, she drew her gaze to his dark-blue coat and grey buckskins, then felt her cheeks warm at the thought of the athletic figure beneath.

"Welcome, ladies. Honoria, Jamie, your great-grandmother sent you a surprise." The earl gestured to the

side of the blanket where two large boxes sat, but his
gaze remained steadfastly on Miss Collins.

The children eagerly ran and fell to their knees, tear-
ing off the tops to see what Lady Hawksworth had given
them. From her box, Honoria lifted out a wooden baton
with a long red streamer. She immediately stood and
ran around, making the ribbon trail after her in long
rippling waves, seeming to float on the breeze.

While his sister was dashing about, Jamie opened his
gift. In the box was a ball and a cricket bat. "How shall
I play cricket without a team of lads?"

Hawksworth, putting aside his thoughts of the lady,
looked at Sir Ethan, and that gentleman gave a brief
nod of his head. "For today, we gentlemen shall be your
team. Come, we shall make a start."

Lady Cora's eyes glittered. "And what are we ladies
to do, while you play Nanny, sir?"

Emily shot a pleased look at Delia, but merely said,
"Come, ladies. Let us join in the fun. While we cannot
play, we can certainly retrieve the ball." When the earl
looked surprised, she added, "Delia and I are not so
fragile as you think, my lord. We have faced the wilds
of an Indian plantation, so a little game of cricket does
not strike fear in our hearts."

The earl grinned; then, placing his arm round Jamie's
shoulders, he led the lad out into the open grass. Lady
Cora's mouth flattened into a thin line as her gaze followed the gentleman. In a voice intended only for
Emily's ears, she remarked, "Well, Miss Collins, I am
certain you are of very hardy stock, but a *lady* does not
dash about on a cricket field. Have you been so long
from Society as not to know what constitutes civilized
behavior?"

Emily rose, saying, "You would be quite amazed, I

think, at how much Society exists in Calcutta, Lady Cora. Yet I think that an afternoon's fun will do little to damage your standing even in London's stricter surroundings."

Lady Cora's chin rose. "My standing allows for a great deal more than yours, Miss Collins. Yet I will forgo the pleasure of dashing about with you and the gentlemen, for I do not think they will admire such hoydenish behavior."

"As you wish, Lady Cora." With that, Emily and Delia moved to where the game was about to begin.

But Lady Cora's prediction proved wrong. Oliver found he liked watching Emily's elegant figure as her muslin gown molded to her when she dashed forward to retrieve the ball. Despite the ladies' lack of skill, fun was had by all the participants. Even the mistakes proved amusing. The earl couldn't remember when he'd felt so carefree, nor laughed with such abandon.

During a lull in the cricket game, Honoria came dashing up shouting, "Uncle, Uncle, look at me."

She ran about the earl with her baton raised high, the red streamer trailing on the breeze. But at that moment Kali jumped and caught the red ribbon in her teeth. The feisty little dog dashed in the opposite direction from Honoria. In an instant, the streamer was wrapped several times around Oliver's legs.

"Nuncheon is served, my lord," Bedows called from the tables.

Oliver couldn't move or he would break Honoria's new gift. "I believe I could use some assistance, Miss Collins."

Emily and Jamie, standing nearby, laughed at his lordship's predicament. The lady called, "I do believe your wards have you where they want you, my lord."

The earl, hands on his hips, laughed. "It would seem so."

Jamie soon convinced Kali to surrender her hold on the ribbon and freed the earl.

Within minutes everyone was gathered back at the blanket where Lady Cora waited, her eyes glinting in anger. "I hope you had a delightful time while I was sitting here all alone."

The earl's eyes gave not a hint to his feelings, but he politely remarked, "I do apologize, my lady. Won't you have one of these marvelous sandwiches that Cook has prepared?"

The lady took the proffered plate, then began to nibble on the sandwich with little enjoyment. She hated being outdoors, she hated being ignored, and most of all she hated children. With noticeable ire, she moved her gown away from Jamie, who'd pushed in to sit beside her with his ugly black mongrel. The boy chattered about the game as he devoured numerous sandwiches with such speed that Lady Cora hoped he might choke.

Instead, the boy was soon finished and asked his uncle if he might be excused. He dashed off to the water's edge, where he found something to amuse himself.

As the adults ate, conversation was sporadic and confined to the excellence of the meal. Then the talk turned to India, and the gentlemen were full of questions about the countryside. But as first Delia, then Emily, spoke of things they remembered, the earl noted that Lady Cora became more sullen to be excluded from the conversation.

Oliver, remembering his promise to his grandmother to be a good host to Lady Cora and feeling guilt at having abandoned her during the game, asked her several questions about the Season. Soon the lady was in high gig, describing all the events she'd attended. She ended with, "I do adore London."

Sir Ethan, fully agreeing with Delia that the marquess's daughter would make a dreadful wife for the earl, decided to put the lady's resolve to a test. "Then why, dear lady, have you come all the way into the country at the height of the Season?"

Lady Cora's aqua gaze moved to the earl. With a coy giggle, she said, "I believe the countess had her reasons for issuing an invitation to my father. I am a great favorite of—"

"Uncle!" Suddenly Jamie interrupted the lady's discourse as he plopped down beside her to announce, "Look what I have found." He opened the box which formerly held his cricket bat and ball. Inside was a veritable army of green frogs in all shapes and sizes. As the curious Kali bounded forward to inspect the treasure, all the creatures attempted to escape the confines of their new prison. The frogs leapt out in all directions, landing in the food, on the blanket and on the ladies.

Ever ready to do her duty, Kali pounced on the nearest frog, sending plates and cups flying. For a moment it seemed as if the blanket were alive with green leapers.

"Get away, get away!" Lady Cora shrieked.

Emily grabbed several of the frogs, trying to keep them from jumping on the terrified woman. "Don't be afraid, my lady. They won't hurt you."

But Lady Cora wasn't listening, only waving her arms and screeching hysterically. To everyone's surprise, she exhibited more agility than one would imagine from her earlier inactivity as she jumped to her feet. The lady swore with the expertise of a groom even while she

batted at two frogs which clung to her gown stubbornly
Before anyone could utter a word of warning, the lad
staggered backward and fell into the lake.

"Lady Cora!" Oliver was on his feet and in the water
in a flash, fearful the lady might come to harm as she
sank under the murky depths. But no sooner had he
helped her to her feet than she jerked her arm free and
stomped out of the water with drooping blond curls
plastered to her wet face, her once white gown now a
grimy green. She came to stand face-to-face with what
she saw as her tormentor, Jamie Carson.

"Everything is ruined! This is all your fault, you little
monster."

With that she drew back her arm and prepared to cuff
the boy. But Emily was there before her, grabbing her
wrist. Quite forgetting that she still held a great green
frog, she pointed the writhing creature in the lady's face
indignantly saying, "You will not hurt this child, Lady
Cora, as long as I am present."

On seeing the frog dangling inches from her nose,
Lady Cora squealed and jumped back.

From behind the stunned group, Lady Hawksworth's
angry voice pierced the afternoon air. "How dare you
try to strike my great-grandson?" All eyes turned to the
countess and her companion, Miss Millet, who'd come
down to visit the picnickers.

Lady Cora, her rage so deep, that she gave little
thought to the circumstances, glared at her ladyship.
"Look at my gown! 'Tis ruined and all you care about
is this hell-begotten puppy." Then she rounded on the
earl, who'd moved back to the shore. "I will have you
know, sir, that I cannot abide all this rural domesticity.
It is well enough to visit one's estate on rare occasions,
but London is where one should spend one's time."

Oliver was heartily tired of Lady Cora. Seeing the outrage and distaste on his grandmother's face, he decided he might at last take action. "You, my lady, may return to your beloved London with my compliments, but I fear that my new responsibilities require that I spend a great deal of time with my delightful young wards in the country."

Lady Cora's face suddenly went ghostly pale as she realized the depths of her mistake. She turned to her one ally, Lady Hawksworth, but the old lady's face appeared as cold as granite. In that instant she knew all was lost. Straightening her back, she announced, "Pray excuse me, but I never remain where I am utterly bored."

With great arrogance, she marched away from the group, but the squashing sound made by her shoes ruined the drama of her exit.

Oliver looked at Emily, who stood with her arm protectively about Jamie. He knew in that instant that he hadn't lied to Lady Cora. This was where he wanted to be. London and all the women of his past no longer held any appeal.

But would he feel the same if it were only he and the children? As his gaze roved over her lovely face, now framed with golden-brown curls loosened by the rigors of the cricket game, he suddenly realized that he wanted Emily Collins to remain a permanent part of the picture.

His grandmother interrupted his thoughts as she moved to stand beside him. "Can you forgive my having mistaken that female for a proper lady? I shudder to think what kind of mother she will make if Halcomb is ever able to bring some unsuspecting fool up to scratch."

He leaned down and kissed his grandmother's flushed cheek. "As long as you agree to leave my affairs in *my* hands."

The lady knew exactly what he referred to and nodded her head in agreement. Then she turned to Emily. "Dear Miss Collins, I cannot thank you enough for protecting my little Jamie from that woman."

Emily was quite unprepared for the lady's change of attitude with regard to her. "My lady, I assure you that the children are as dear to Delia and me as they are to your family."

Jamie, distracted by Lady Cora's near assault, suddenly remembered that all his captives were escaping back to the lake and began to dash about to return as many as possible and confine them in the box. Soon everyone, save the countess and Miss Millet, had joined him. Afterward, Oliver struggled to convince the lad that the frogs would be better outdoors than in the nursery and was forced to appeal to Emily and Delia. A compromise was soon found. The frogs would be placed in the small fountain in the knot garden near the castle for the time being.

Sir Ethan, eyeing his friend's sodden condition, announced that the children would be in need of a new guardian if Oliver continued to stand around wearing wet clothing in the cool air.

The earl offered his grandmother and Miss Millet each an arm and led them back to the castle as Emily and Delia helped the children gather their hats, new toys and pets. Sir Ethan remained behind to escort the younger ladies.

While the children ran ahead, the baronet offered an arm to each lady. As they made their way back to the castle, Delia quietly thanked the gentleman for helping arrange the picnic and thus saving the children from having Lady Cora as an aunt.

Sir Ethan laughed. "Oh, I had little to do with it, lass. 'Twas the lady who did in her own chances to be the new countess. I was hesitant to intrude into my friend's affairs, but I cannot say I am unhappy at the results. One can see she will make a dreadful wife."

Emily couldn't contain her curiosity. "How did Lord Hawksworth come to contemplate such a termagant for a bride?"

The baronet considered the question for a moment. Not thinking it proper to discuss his friend's private affairs with others, he merely said, "On the surface, the lass has what most gentlemen in Society want, Miss Collins. Lineage, beauty and of course the one thing that might make up for the lack of everything else—a fortune."

The words sent a cold chill down Emily's spine. Was her fortune going to be some prize that gentlemen vied for, caring little about her? The prospect certainly made a Season in London less appealing. Perhaps Delia was correct; the fewer people who knew of her inheritance, the better.

They reached the castle where the earl, still in his wet clothes, awaited them alone, the countess having retired to her rooms. There was a look in his eyes that sent her heart racing.

"May I have a word with you, Miss Collins?"

Sir Ethan suggested that he and Delia see the children back to their nurse. Emily was aware of the worry in her friend's eyes at the prospect of leaving her alone with the earl.

"I shall only be a moment." Then she followed the earl into the library.

He moved near the fire, and Emily joined him there. When his gaze met hers, time seemed to stand still. There was a magnetism in his blue eyes that sent her senses reeling. Their mesmerized gazes remained locked, and the only sound in the room was the crackling of the fire. The muted conversation of passing servants in the hall seemed to bring the earl from his trance, but there was a huskiness in his voice. "I merely wanted to thank you for what you did in protecting my nephew."

As every nerve in her body seemed to tingle at his look, Emily struggled to keep her thoughts on the conversation. "My lord, I hope you are not too disappointed to discover Lady Cora's shortcomings."

Oliver was amazed at the depth of his feelings for the woman before him. He struggled to keep his desire for Emily in check. He wanted to crush her to him and devour her, but she was not some practiced mistress, only an innocent in the ways of love. Instead he gave in to impulse only to the extent of tracing his finger along her jawline before lifting her chin. "I discovered a great deal more than that today, my dear."

Emily's heart raced as she took his meaning; then the earl's mouth covered hers. She knew she should be outraged that he'd taken such a liberty, but instead she surrendered herself freely to the passion in his kiss. She'd tried to keep from falling victim to his charms, but when his lips touched hers, she knew she was lost. She was in love with Oliver Carson.

A knock sounded at the door. Startled, the pair drew apart. Emily again gazed up into the blue eyes of the earl and trembled, but she wasn't certain if it was from fear of her own raging emotions or that he didn't love her and was merely amusing himself, as rakes were wont to do.

Hawksworth bade the intruder to enter in a hoarse tone, and a servant stepped into the library to inform his lordship that his grandmother had ordered him out of his wet clothes at once or he would fall ill.

Emily was suddenly embarrassed at her wanton conduct. "You must do as your grandmother bids, my lord." With that she hurried from the room, her thoughts in a whirl.

Oliver cursed his grandmother for once again interfering in his affairs, but went up to get more comfortable even as his thoughts dwelled on Emily Collins.

The distracted earl scarcely had thirty minutes to change before he learned that Lord Halcomb's carriage was at the door and about to depart. Glad to be rid of the pair, but knowing his duty as a host, he hurried down to exchange stilted farewells. He might have saved himself the time, for neither the lady nor her father was in a mood fit for man or beast.

With an angry shout, Lord Halcomb ordered his coachman to spring 'em, and the coach bowled away from Hawk's Lair. Bedows closed the door as he muttered, "Good riddance," to which Oliver silently agreed, but he merely informed the butler to tell Sir Ethan he might be found in the library.

The earl settled behind his desk, but was in no humor to look at the accounts Mr. Grant had left. His mind returned to the earlier kiss. He was in love with the contrary, managing Emily Collins. The kiss had only confirmed what he knew—he wanted her. He had wanted her from her early days at the castle, but now it was more than mere physical desire. She had stirred his blood as no other woman ever had. True, it was often in anger, but it had only made him determined to gain the upper hand in the next encounter. Life would never run smoothly with Emily. He was certain they would argue over most matters, but he wanted her to be his wife, to share his life and the lives of his wards.

At the thought of proposing to Emily, his mind moved to Lady Hawksworth and all her plans. There could be little doubt that despite his grandmother's softening attitude, she would be resistant to a female who lacked the aristocratic lineage and vast fortune of Lady Cora While Oliver knew little of Emily's history save that she came from a genteel family from Warwickshire, he'd gleaned the information that she was an orphan whose late uncle had run an indigo plantation in the India. Doubtless the heirs had sent her packing upon inheriting, but she seemed reluctant to speak of other members of her family.

The sounds of a carriage arriving at the castle brought Oliver from his musing. Concerned that the marquess had returned for some reason, the earl rose and opened the library door, prepared to immediately handle any matter concerning Halcomb or his daughter.

Unobserved, he watched in amazement as a rail-thin man with blunt features, who was dressed in an ill-fitting coat of brown superfine, pushed his way past the butler. A rotund little woman in a dark green traveling gown and two young people—the elder male and the other female—hovered in the doorway as if fearful to cross the threshold. The intrusive gentleman scanned the contents of the Great Hall as if he were taking an inventory before he querulously announced, "I demand to see the Earl of Hawksworth at once, my good man."

Bedows was not in the least intimidated. "If you have a card, sir, I shall take it to my master to see if he is at home."

The man shook his cane at the servant. "I'll not be barred from a house where my niece is in residence. If that rake ain't at home, then inform Miss Collins that her family has come to welcome her back into the bosom of her family."

Oliver stifled a groan. Every line in the stranger's posture spoke his unhappiness at finding his young relative at Hawk's Lair. There could be little doubt the man was fully aware of Oliver's reputation.

Unfortunately, there was little hope of avoiding contact with Emily's relations, since he fully intended to marry her. Oliver closed the door and returned to his desk, where Bedows found him some moments later. The earl took the card and tossed it to his desk after a brief glance. "Show them in, Bedows, and inform Miss Collins of their arrival."

Ten

In her private drawing room, Emily stood before the windows, her fingers lingering on her lips as she remembered the searing kiss in the library. The earl's touch had sent her senses reeling, but with distance between them, she must think more rationally. She couldn't allow herself to hope for much beyond a dalliance on the gentleman's part. While she might foolishly harbor dreams of marriage, perhaps the earl's ideal of a proper wife was someone of Lady Cora's stamp— aristocratic, sophisticated and wealthy.

Then she remembered the baronet's words that a fortune would make most gentlemen forget the lack of the former qualities. Well, she wouldn't be wed merely for her money.

Yet still she clung to the idea that perhaps Lord Hawksworth had truly fallen in love with her. That he intended to make her an offer. She'd been careful not to mention the fortune she'd inherited. Could he have kissed her in such a manner without some deep feeling?

At that moment Delia entered. "The children are all safely back with Mrs. Waters." Then, seeing the look on Emily's face, she came to her, saying, "What did the earl wish to speak with you about?"

Emily shrugged, but felt her cheeks warm. "Lord Hawksworth wanted to thank me for protecting Jamie from Lady Cora's wrath."

"Then why do you seem so . . . distressed?"

With a tight laugh, Emily moved to sit in a chair near the fire. "Don't be silly. I am merely tired and a bit flushed from all the outdoor activity."

Delia joined her friend, still doubtful of her mood. She made an effort to keep the conversation light by speaking of the children and the pleasantries of the afternoon before Lady Cora's tantrum.

A knock sounded on the door, startling the ladies. Upon entering, Bedows announced, "Miss Collins, a Mr. Joshua Collins and his family have arrived."

At once Emily turned to Delia, knowing only she would have known where to correspond with Emily's relations. "What have you done?"

The widow bit at her lip. "I thought it for the best, my dear. You are young and fabulously wealthy. You heard what Sir Ethan said this afternoon. You will be attracting every fortune hunter in England when word gets about that a new heiress has arrived. You will need the protection of a family. I cannot bear to think of anything bad happening to you." Delia wisely refrained from mentioning her fears about the earl, knowing her employer's headstrong nature.

A thought suddenly flashed through Emily's mind that she might need someone to protect her from her own family. But having not seen them in years, she knew she might be doing them an injustice.

"You know they would not have me all those years ago after my parents died." With a sigh at the old hurt, Emily took note of the contrite expression on Delia's face. "Don't worry. I shall go down and welcome them.

Who knows, they may be much improved in the intervening years."

She rose and announced, "Bedows, I must change my gown first, then I shall join my relatives." Without another word, she went to change and prepare herself for a meeting with people she thought never to see again.

Determined to be civil despite Mr. Collins's belligerent attitude in the hall, Oliver extended his hand to the man when he marched into the library. "Good afternoon, sir. I am Hawksworth. 'Tis a pleasure to meet Miss Collins's family."

That gentleman was a bit taken aback by Lord Hawksworth's friendly attitude, for it was not what he'd heard upon making enquiries about the earl after receiving Mrs. Keaton's letter. In truth, Squire Collins had been much distressed to learn that his niece had fallen into the clutches of a hardened rake—although his feelings had little to do with Emily, barely remembering her as more than a tearful waif at his brother's and sister-in-law's funeral, and a great deal to do with the fortune she'd inherited.

He eyed the earl speculatively, then decided there was no reason to alienate such a powerful lord. The squire was certain that all he need do was exercise his power as head of the family and he would soon have the girl away from Hawksworth and under his control. The gentleman quickly introduced himself, his wife and his children, then got down to the matter which was so urgent.

"We have only just learned of our beloved niece's return from the Indies and hurried to bring her back to Warwickshire. We would like to greet her on her much-anticipated return."

"Of course. I am certain she will be delighted. I have already sent word of your arrival. She should be here any moment. May I offer some refreshments while you wait?"

A delighted smile lit Mrs. Collins's round face. "Oh, that would do nicely, my lord, for we were in such a hurry to arrive that we had only a paltry fare at a shabby little inn on the road."

Mr. Collins frowned at his wife and she fell silent, a contrite look on her countenance. Mr. Roland Collins inquired about a collection of snuffboxes that were displayed on a small table in the corner, seemingly little interested in greeting his cousin.

Oliver scanned the faces of the group in front of him as all but Roland took their seats before the fire to await Emily. Mrs. Collins appeared to be one of those women with little to say save for parroting her husband's views, as she presently sat with a vacant look in her eyes, her hands folded. Mr. Roland Collins was a handsome young man who appeared almost foppish, while Miss Bettina Collins was plain and inclined to the dowdy plumpness of her mother. But where the mother looked vacuous, the daughter's intelligence was evident in lively green eyes which watched her father with what could only be described as distaste.

The arrival of the Collinses was a puzzle to Oliver. While Emily had spoken lovingly of her late Uncle Nathaniel, she'd made no mention of any English relations. In truth, Oliver had the impression she had none, or at least none with whom she wished to renew ties.

The tea tray came long before Emily. As Bedows served, Mr. Collins watched Oliver with dark, shifty eyes. Mrs. Collins's attention was riveted on the selection of cakes and sandwiches on the silver tray, but the son seemed more interested in inspecting the contents of the room than eating as he picked up one item after another to examine. Miss Bettina sat worrying her bottom lip as if some great problem weighed upon her.

Oliver was suddenly reminded of ferrets when his gaze roved from Mr. Collins to his son as their sharp features seemed to take in everything. Clearly Emily took after her mother's family.

At last the awaited lady entered the library. She cast a shy, yet intimate smile in Oliver's direction before turning her gaze on her uncle. Then such a bleak look settled in her amber eyes that Oliver wanted to go to her and hold her in his arms, but he was certain she wouldn't welcome such conduct in front of her relatives. Instead he merely said, "Miss Collins, your family has come to greet you."

She stood stiff and unyielding as the Collinses all trooped forward to give her a welcoming kiss. Only Bettina sounded genuine when she said, "Welcome home, Cousin."

Emily's tone was anything but welcoming to Mr. Collins. "Uncle Joshua, you needn't have come all the way to Somerset. I am certain we would have encountered one another in Town . . . sooner or later."

"Don't be ridiculous, my dear child. It's been nearly fifteen years since we last saw you. We have worried ourselves sick about you since we received word of your Uncle Nate's passing and you all alone in that heathen land to deal with all those financial matters of selling the plantation. Why, Roland even suggested he might come out and escort you back to England."

The young man gave her an engaging smile. "It

would have been my great honor to have rendered such a service, Cousin." He then gave a practiced bow.

Emily's gaze swept her young cousin, whom she remembered as a detestable brat who'd carried tales about her to Uncle Joshua during her brief stay at their home. She took in pomaded blond curls, a purple coat and red waistcoat with large gold buttons and four fobs dangling at his waist. Her opinion was that the young dandy probably couldn't get himself across the street without help, much less out to Calcutta.

But manners won out over distaste. "As you can see, sir, there was no need for such worry. My dear Uncle Nate's health was such in later years that I handled much of the day-to-day workings of the plantation. I am quite used to managing my own affairs."

Joshua Collins didn't like what he saw in his niece. This was not the same shy and frightened child of long ago. She had grown into one of those females who believed that balderdash the Wollstonecraft creature had written about. Women being able to handle their own affairs—ha!

He would have to warn Roland to go slowly or all their plans would be for naught. But at present he must cozen this foolish child into believing he agreed with her.

"Well, my dear, we are duly impressed." The squire gave a broad grin, exposing yellowed teeth. "But now you are home, and Roland and I are fully prepared to advise you on all matters. There is nothing like a gentleman's experience when making decisions."

"I assure you, Uncle, there is no need." Emily's expression was unyielding.

Mr. Collins was at a standstill. How was he to control this stubborn miss? As his silence lengthened, his wife inadvertently aided him when she took note of the lull in conversation. Oblivious to much of the by-play between uncle and niece, she put down the sticky bun she was enjoying to timidly inquire, "My dear, I am puzzled as to why you have lingered here in Somerset when your uncle has been eagerly awaiting you in Coventry."

"Was he?" Emily asked, doubtfully. "That seems surprising, since no one was eager for my presence so many years ago."

With the cunning of most connivers, the squire realized what troubled his niece. The chit was still piqued about that business when only Ashton had been willing to take an orphan. Convinced he could turn her around, he stepped to her, taking her hand. In his best imitation of familial concern, he said, "Child, if my finances had been better at the time your father died, I would have welcomed you to Twin Oaks, but I was nearly in Dun Territory. Besides, that was all long ago and best forgotten. You are back with us at last, and we are most eager to hear about your life in the Indies."

Oliver watched the play of emotion on Emily's lovely face. Clearly there was some unhappy history between the pair, but he thought Emily needed some time to cope with meeting her family again after so many years. She seemed at a loss for words.

The earl decided to explain Emily's extended stay at the castle. "Miss Collins has been helping my wards, whom she and Mrs. Keaton so kindly brought from Calcutta, to become established in their new home."

The squire's small black eyes narrowed as he looked at the earl; then he turned back to Emily. "As I remember, you always did have a kind heart, my dear. And have the children been settled to your satisfaction?"

Emily straightened defiantly. "Why, no, Uncle. Lord Hawksworth and I still must interview applicants for a governess." Then she looked at Oliver, and her face softened to a smile.

"Very well, my dear." Mr. Collins glared at the earl truculently. "But we have no intention of leaving Somerset without you."

Oliver knew what was expected and manners demanded. "Then you and your family must stay at Hawk's Lair until Miss Collins is ready to leave." He knew it would not do to inform them that he hoped she would never depart while still Miss Collins, but until he secured her hand he would hold his peace.

Mr. Collins smiled with satisfaction. He had his foot in the door of Emily's life. Roland would have to get to work on charming his cousin at once, for there was something in the way his niece looked at the earl that didn't bode well for the squire's family fortunes.

Hawksworth rang for the butler, and rooms were quickly prepared for the Collinses. The earl informed them that dinner would be served at eight; then Emily and her family left for their rooms. To his surprise, Miss Bettina Collins lingered in her seat, then came to stand beside him after her family had departed the room.

In a whispered undertone, she pleaded, "My lord, are you truly my cousin's friend?"

Surprised, Oliver looked at the strange girl. "I hope to be more than just a friend one day, Miss Bettina."

The young lady seemed to relax a bit, then pushed a small folded note into his hand. Without another word, she hurried from the library to join her family.

Curious, Oliver opened the small missive. *I must*

speak with you at once. Send a servant for me in exactly twenty minutes.

What melodramatic nonsense was this? Oliver wondered. But he was certain that it concerned Emily, and therefore he would play Miss Bettina's little game.

The meeting of Miss Bettina Collins and Lord Hawksworth took place some twenty minutes later in the Long Gallery. Oliver knew that should they be discovered by anyone, he might use the pretext of showing the young miss the family portraits to excuse the impropriety of such a meeting.

He observed her closely as she followed Bedows down the narrow room towards him. She had changed into an ecru muslin evening gown with heavy use of Brussels lace and green ribbon at the bodice and sleeves. The garment, with three rows of ruffles at the hem, did little to flatter her full figure. He knew little of feminine apparel, but was certain that the lady would have appeared better in a simply cut dress.

Her plain face was a picture of concern as she drew to a halt, then waited for the servant to depart before breathlessly saying, "We must hurry or my father will know I have spoken to you, my lord."

Oliver arched one brow. "What do you wish to tell me, Miss Bettina?"

She threw a nervous glance over her shoulder to make certain they were unobserved. "My father and brother mean my cousin no good, my lord."

"Are you saying they intend her harm?" The earl's hands drew into fists at the thought.

"Nothing like that, sir. My father would never risk his neck in such a way, and Roland gets quite ill at the least sight of blood. No, their intention is to take her back to Twin Oaks and browbeat her into marrying Roland."

"Browbeat! Miss Collins?" Oliver threw back his head and laughed heartily.

" 'Tis no laughing matter, my lord. You do not know my father. He may not be a murderer, but one very often wishes to be dead when he is giving one a devilish bad time."

Oliver stifled his laughter, not wishing to belittle the girl's worries. "Child, I don't mean to take what you say lightly, but if there is anyone less likely to be browbeaten than your cousin, I am sure I do not know them. She is a lady who very much knows her own mind. Let me assure you that Miss Collins is a very sensible and capable female."

But Bettina was not easily swayed by the earl's assurances. " 'tis plain that you admire her, sir. Yet I know my father well. He is determined to make certain that the fortune Nathaniel Ashton left his niece will not get away from him."

"Fortune?" Oliver's dark brows drew together. "Are you telling me Miss Emily Collins is an heiress?"

Bettina's green eyes grew wide. "You did not know, sir, and yet you wished to marry her? It must be love, indeed. Yes, there is a fortune. My father estimates that Emily has inherited close to a hundred thousand pounds from her uncle."

Suddenly what the young lady had been telling him took on new meaning. With such a fortune at stake, Bettina might be underestimating the drastic measures her father might employ to get his hands on such a prize.

He eyed the young lady curiously. "Why have you chosen to tell me and not your cousin?"

"I had intended to tell Emily, but it was clear to me from the outset that she views us as complete strangers. I cannot blame her, for she was shipped off to the Indies all those years ago because she was penniless, no matter what Papa may now say. Besides, I was certain a man could thwart my father's plans much better than a lone female."

Oliver again grew silent. He was curious why a young woman who might benefit from such a plan would be the very one to expose her father's plot. "Why are you helping your cousin? You know her as little as she knows you."

The young lady looked down at her gloved hands. When she looked back at the earl, there was such bitterness in her green eyes that he was startled. "My father and brother care for nothing but money. Over a year ago my brother learned that I had formed an attachment with our curate and he with me. Roland informed my father. They went to the baron who owned the living and saw to it that the kindest man I ever knew lost his position. Without my knowledge, he was told he would never be allowed to marry me and was ordered from the shire. I have not seen him since." She gave a deep sigh as her eyes shimmered with unshed tears. "I do not want them to ruin Emily's life the way they did mine."

Miss Bettina's motives were clear in her mind, but the earl suspected there was a bit of revenge against her family mixed with her desire to help Emily. Still, without a second thought, he asked, "What was this curate's name?"

"Mr. Darnell Logan." She spoke the name with reverence.

The earl's primary concern was for Emily at the moment, but after the service this plain young lady had rendered him, he was determined to see if he could find her curate for her. He leaned over and gave the girl a kiss on the cheek. "You have done your cousin a great service by telling me all this, Miss Bettina. I shall be certain to tell her about it some day after she is my bride. Do not give up hope of your curate. Now hurry along to the Blue Drawing Room and I shall see you there later."

Oliver watched as the girl hurried back up the Long Gallery. He knew he mustn't delay. Joshua Collins had dubious intentions which threatened the welfare of the woman he loved, and Oliver fully intended to stop him. He would propose to Emily this very night and secure his position to protect her. With that he strode purposefully towards the Blue Drawing Room.

But the earl had not reckoned with the tenacity of Mr. Collins and his son. The two gentlemen had positioned themselves on either side of Emily as she waited for the others to arrive. It was as if they'd formed a guard around their young relative to prevent her from having private conversation with any save themselves. To all observers, the gentlemen appeared rapt and interested in all Emily had to say of her fifteen years in the Indies, but for Oliver their every move appeared calculated to keep him from her.

It wasn't until after dinner, when the countess announced that she wished to speak with Oliver in the library about the children, that everyone began to say their good nights and the earl got his chance. He was at last able to secure Emily's hand in a private moment, only to be frustrated by his grandmother's summons. He knew that he would be unable to speak with Emily that evening. So in a soft tone for her ears only, he asked, "Might I have a word with you in the library at nine on the morrow?"

The lady smiled and nodded her head before her hovering relations drew her upstairs with them. Oliver bade Sir Ethan good night, apologizing for such an early evening, but the gentleman was understanding, saying he could use a good night's rest before he strode off up the stairs.

The earl's gaze followed Emily until she disappeared from sight. A part of him wanted to go to her private parlor and lay his heart at her feet, but his grandmother's words echoed in his head—that there must be no hint of impropriety to mar his proposal of marriage since his reputation was already so tainted. He would wait until the morrow.

When the sounds of his guests' footsteps had faded, he joined his grandmother in the library. Closing the door, he turned and inquired, "Is there a problem with the children, madam?"

"How soon before you are able to hire a governess?" the old lady asked impatiently from her seat before the fire.

The earl moved to stand at the mantel. "I have been expecting the agency to send applicants any day. Is there suddenly some hurry?"

" 'Tis these dreadful people, the Collinses." Seeing the look on her grandson's face, she knew at once the direction his thoughts had taken. With a shake of her head, she added, "Oh, I don't mean Miss Emily Collins, for she is an admirable enough young female. But until you hire a governess, she is quite determined to stay nd assist you. That means her disreputable relations ntend to remain fawning on the chit as if she were 'rincess Charlotte."

Oliver knew there was no time like the present to >reak the news to his grandmother. "Madam, I know >f all your plans for me, but I have some of my own. I have decided to ask Miss Collins to marry me."

The old lady's eyes grew round with distress. "Marry some . . . young woman who has little to offer? I like he gel, but she cannot be the new countess. Why, it would be the height of foolishness, Oliver, when there are any number of titled young females in Town who would willingly become your bride and enhance your fortune at the same time."

"Titles and fortunes are of no consequence to me, Grandmother. I love Emily."

"Love! Marriage is no time to be thinking about such maudlin nonsense. Love is for silly schoolgirls and poets. The rest of us do our duty to our names and our families by marrying for advantage."

The earl had known how it would be when he tried to make the dowager understand his feelings for Emily. He'd had the lecture on what constituted a proper bride too many times over the years. Still, he'd hoped to convince his grandparent that none of the things which were so important to Society mattered to him. But it was clear that the countess would not be swayed by sentimentality or romance. So he took the simplest route to convince her that Emily would be a proper bride.

"Clearly the reason for Miss Collins's relations sudden appearance has not occurred to you. She has returned from the Indies an heiress."

"How do you know she is an heiress? It might be a a hum to entice you to marry her."

"Emily has not spoken of the matter. 'Twas Miss Be tina Collins who informed me that it was the reason h father has come to whisk Emily away from here. H intends to marry her to that coxcomb, Roland."

A thoughtful expression settled on the countess's line face. Emily Collins was not at all the kind of woma she would have expected an Earl of Hawksworth marry. She herself had been a reigning beauty with vast fortune, as had Oliver's mother. How was it tha Oliver had settled on such a modest-looking female Clearly the lady's fortune had little to do with h choice, since he'd only just learned of it.

She watched her grandson's resolute expression. H had made his choice. Nora held little hope that sh could change his mind. She considered the matter care fully. While Miss Collins didn't have a title or ancie lineage, she appeared to have a fortune, which mad her acceptable in the strictest sense. Then the memor of the lady's fierce defense of young Jamie came mind. The countess knew the young lady had somethin more than most young ladies—she had heart, and tha would be best for the future of Jamie, Honoria an Wesley.

"So, this Uncle Nathaniel she speaks of was a nabo Well, well, that changes things, dear boy." Seeing a angry glint leap into the earl's eyes, the dowager chucl led. "Don't take that attitude with me, my boy. I wa only doing what has been done throughout the ages, an that is to see to the best interest of the family with a alliance. For myself, I shall like having Miss Collins a a granddaughter-in-law, and if a fortune comes with he I am well satisfied."

With that Oliver knew he would have to be content. He informed the countess of his intention to propose the following morning. The lady, once she'd accepted the inevitable, began to discuss the advantages to the wedding taking place at the castle chapel versus at St George's in London.

While the pair in the library continued to argue over the details, a figure stealthily crept away from the door. Roland Collins had stolen back down the stairs after most had retired for the night, fully intending to glean a few simple trinkets to lighten the burden of his debt. After all, the earl had so much and he so little due to his clutch-fisted father. But the sounds of voices had lured him to the library door, and his eavesdropping had paid off better than a few paltry snuffboxes might. He hurried up the stairs to tell his father that drastic action would have to be taken or Emily's fortune would be lost to them forever. He would also make certain his father punished Bettina for her loose tongue.

Eleven

Emily rose early the following morning unable to re press the excitement she was feeling. Those final tw minutes in the Blue Drawing Room with the earl hole ing her hand had made up for the entire evening of boredom fending off the Collinses. She was looking for ward to being with the earl without her dreadful rela tives hovering about. She wondered what he wished speak to her about, then assumed he had heard from the agency regarding a governess for the children.

Dressed in a simple pink morning gown trimmed with rose-colored ribbons, she entered her small sitting room but to her surprise, she found Delia was there before her. Her companion paced the Oriental rug before the fire, halting at the sight of her employer.

"Oh, Emily, I feel I must do something to make u for my dreadful mistake."

"Mistake? You mean writing to Uncle Joshua?"

Delia nodded. "I am not certain which one, your un cle or your cousin, I find the more detestable with a their toadeating and feigned interest in your experience after practically throwing you out into the world. Ha I any idea they would prove such pushing people, would never have informed them of our location. Eve

Sir Ethan says that Roland appears a dirty dish if ever he saw one and your uncle not much better. You would have every right to dismiss me—send me away for what I have done to you."

Emily took her companion's fidgeting hands between her own. "What's done is done, my dear. You needn't worry about me. I fully intend to inform my uncle that he and his family's presence are not needed at Hawk's Lair and that furthermore I shall not be returning to Twin Oaks with the Collinses."

The widow nodded her head in agreement, but still a frown remained on her pretty face. "I don't think the gentleman will go easily. No doubt he is aware you inherited Mr. Ashton's wealth and thinks to gain control of the funds. His timid wife and daughter are evidence of his domination, my dear. He will intimidate you to yield to his wishes. I would guess he is much used to having his own way within the family."

"He may try, but I am made of sterner stuff. Do not worry about the matter anymore. I want to speak of another—"

Just then an urgent knocking sounded on the door. The ladies exchanged a puzzled look before Emily called for the visitor to enter.

Joshua Collins stepped into the room. His features were schooled into an expression of great consternation.

"Ah, Uncle, you are just the man I wished to see."

"Did you?" The gentleman was wary. He'd seen little to convince him that Emily Collins was warming to her relatives. Was he too late to do anything about what Roland had told him last night? He forged ahead with the plan he and his son had devised. "Well, my dear, I'm not certain you will be so happy to see me when

I have told you what dreadful thing I have learned. May we speak in private?"

The squire gave Delia a haughty look, as if she were an intruder, but Emily took her friend's hand. "I can handle matters here. Go and take the air, for it is very fine this morning. I shall join you later."

After Mrs. Keaton was gone, Emily suggested they be seated. She noted the time on the Ormulu clock, making certain she would not miss her meeting with Oliver at nine. "What have you to tell me, sir?"

Mr. Collins made a great show of reluctance. "I know that you have come to admire the earl and Lady Hawksworth, but I fear they mean to use you badly."

Doubtful, but willing to let the man have his say, Emily responded, "In what way, Uncle?"

"This shall be very hard for you to hear, my dear niece, but Roland overheard the two discussing the earl proposing marriage to you this very day to gain your fortune."

Emily's heart froze at that moment. How had the earl learned of her fortune? Was a marriage proposal the reason behind his lordship's interest in seeing her this morning? Or was this some ruse on her uncle's part? She scanned his lined face, but there was such a look of glee in the depth of his dark eyes that it was evident he wasn't fabricating the story. Roland had been eavesdropping.

The realization of the earl's plan sent a sharp pain through her chest. But she refused to allow her uncle to see the hurt his tale had brought. With a great effort at nonchalance, she calmly arched a brow. "And was Cousin Roland's ear pressed to a door at the time?"

Mr. Collins's face flushed deep red, showing that she had struck the truth. He waved a hand dismissively.

"That is of no importance, child. What is important is that Lord Hawksworth and his grandmother were cold-heartedly discussing a marriage to enhance his coffers. You may be a little nobody in their eyes, but even a rake won't whistle a hundred thousand pounds down the wind over the lack of pedigree."

The pain in Emily's chest grew. All her worst fears were coming to pass. What she wanted most was to go to her bedchamber and weep, but she still had to deal with her uncle. She rose on unsteady limbs and walked to the window in an attempt to gain control of her emotions. At last she looked back at the gentleman who watched her eagerly. "And how does the earl's plan differ from yours, sir?"

The gentleman straightened at her suggestion that his motives were no better. "Whatever do you mean? *We* are family."

"Uncle, you forgot that fifteen years ago. 'Tis amazing how a fortune has suddenly revived the familial feelings which were missing for a frightened and penniless orphan."

"I explained that—"

"So you did. And you were right. All that is in the past. I am no longer frightened or penniless and well able to handle all my own affairs, be they financial or . . . ones of the heart." Her voice caught on the last word. She struggled to regain her composure. "You and your family should return to Warwickshire. I have informed my solicitor of my wish to purchase my *own* home. For the time being, it is my intention to go to London and establish a residence with Mrs. Keaton and to enjoy the delights of the Season."

Mr. Collins sputtered, "I won't have—"

Emily's amber eyes glittered. "*You won't have*, sir?

You have nothing to say about my affairs. I am five and twenty, not a child to be ordered to the Indies at your whim. You think you can completely ignore me all those years and now expect to command my obedience?"

With that she turned her back to him. "Pray, gather your family and return to Twin Oaks, sir. There is nothing here for you."

Joshua Collins knew he'd been a fool. He'd put the destitute child from his mind once he'd pushed her responsibility onto Nathaniel Ashton's shoulders, never realizing the girl might come back an heiress when Mrs. Ashton proved barren. Despite their best efforts, she would have none of her family or, more important, of Roland. There was no way to erase the years of mistakes.

With shoulders sagging in defeat, he walked to the door. But like most men of his stamp, within minutes he had decided that he would send Roland to London to try his luck again. It would cost a fortune, but they couldn't give up so easily. At least his plan had put an end to any ideas Hawksworth may have had to wed the girl, for despite her best efforts to conceal her emotions, Mr. Collins was convinced his niece believed his altered story of the truth and would refuse the gentleman. With that he departed the chamber and hurried to speak with his son.

Still at the window, Emily stood frozen as she heard the door close. Every fiber of her being wanted her to rush back to her room and give in to her overwhelming despair. The earl wanted to marry her, but for the wrong reason.

She knew she couldn't give in to her wretchedness. She still had to face the earl. Then she and Delia must depart at once. She couldn't stay at Hawk's Lair knowing she loved Oliver, while he was merely looking for a wealthy wife. She would go through with her plan to have her solicitor quietly purchase a nearby property, but would always make certain the earl was not in residence before she and Delia paid a visit to the children.

With that she returned to her room and rang for the maid and Swarup. They must begin packing at once. She wanted to be on the road before noon.

Oliver paused before the lone mirror in the library and straightened the folds of his cravat. For some reason his nervous fingers only seemed to further disturb the intricate arrangement. He'd never before had difficulty in tying his neckcloth, but today he'd been all thumbs, ruining three of the starched ties before finally settling for his current style, the Waterfall.

The sound of a knock made him start; then he turned and smiled, knowing it could only be Emily. He called for her to enter and moved across the room to greet her, but his steps faltered as the door opened and he saw the look on her face. Something was wrong.

"Is there some problem, my dear?"

"No, my lord, I have merely come to inform you that Mrs. Keaton and I intend to depart for London this morning." Her tone was clipped and impersonal.

Oliver was stunned. She stared at him as if he were a stranger. This was not the same woman he'd kissed in the library only a day ago, not the woman who'd smiled at him so intimately last night. "What has happened?"

Emily looked down at the floor, shuttering her eyes from the earl. "Nothing, my lord. I have come to realize that Delia and I have remained too long in Somerset when we have matters in London which need tending to."

Nothing was going as Oliver had planned. She was upset and he didn't know why. He knew that if he could just get her to hear him out all would change. "My dear Miss Collins . . ." His voice softened to a husky whisper. "My dear Emily, I know not what has caused you to wish to leave Hawk's Lair, but I can only assume it has to do with your uncle. Pray tell me what troubles you."

"Sir, do not assume anything about me." Her amber gaze flew up to glare at him in anger.

She made to turn, but Oliver, desperate to comprehend what was wrong, grabbed her shoulders. "Listen to me, my dear. I don't understand what has occurred, I only know that I don't want you to leave." Seeing no softening in her expression, he lost his patience. "For heaven's sake, I want to marry you, Emily."

Emily closed her eyes but a moment as the pain of his declaration surged through her. His very words confirmed everything her uncle had said. How else would he have known that the earl would propose today?

Opening her eyes, she stared at a button on his waistcoat, unable to look at his handsome face. "Do you, sir? Are you certain you have not been precipitous? 'Twas only two days ago you were wanting to marry Lady Cora. Perhaps if you wait another day or so, you will want to marry someone else."

The earl's back stiffened at the insult and his hands fell away from her shoulders. "Is that what you think of me? That I am some gadabout flitting from woman to woman? Let me assure you that I never wished to marry Lady Cora Lane."

"Was she not led to believe that you intended to make her an offer?" Emily ventured a peek at his face and the grimness was frightening.

"Not by me, but I will not deny that before I met you, I did consider the lady as a possible bride." He paused and looked at her intently. "Emily, do not mistake the machinations of my grandmother for some great romance. I had never even been introduced to Lady Cora before she arrived at the castle."

The earl couldn't know that his statement only made it worse for him. In Emily's mind it only confirmed that he was willing to marry where there was no love as long as the female possessed money and gentility.

"Well, my lord, I believe it is proper for me to thank you for the kindness of your offer. But I must refuse, for I—"

"Proper, kindness!" The earl suddenly grabbed Emily's shoulders and pulled her to his chest. Her gaze flew up to his, and the fierce light in his eyes frightened her. "Proper be damned, woman. Have you not heard a word I've said? I'm trying to tell you what's in my heart, but perhaps I should show you."

With that Oliver's mouth covered hers hungrily. Despite the fact that his kiss was punishing and angry, Emily experienced the rush of all the feeling his first embrace had engendered—want and need. But deep in the back of her mind, she recalled that this man was a notorious rake. He was practiced in the art of love. She mustn't allow him to sweep her away on a tide of passion only to recover and discover that once his lust was sated, she would be little more than a convenience to him.

She broke free from his arms, breathless but determined to do what she knew she must. "How dare you, sir! Have you not been listening to me? I have refused your offer. Do you intend to compromise me to get your way?"

Her words were like a slap in the face to Oliver. He knew he'd behaved like a cad, but he'd only meant to get through that wall she'd built between them. He loved her, but it appeared he'd been mistaken in her feelings for him. He'd opened his heart to her, and she'd rejected him. Hurt and angry at her cold response, he snapped, "Miss Collins, you must forgive my ungentlemanly conduct. You have my word it will not occur again while you remain under my roof."

Something in his tone touched her heart; then she stiffened her resolve not to be his and his grandmother's pawn. "Well, my lord, I shall not put too much of a strain on you since I intend to leave within the hour." So saying, she turned and exited the library.

Oliver stood staring at the door as he heard the lady's footsteps fading. Never before had he been on the receiving end of a rejection. He suddenly remembered all the ladies through the years who'd declared they loved him and whom he'd walked away from. For the first time he understood what they might have suffered if their words of love were true. Was God punishing him by allowing him to fall in love with a woman who wanted no part of him? What had happened to change her so greatly?

At that moment his mind, so full of hurt and anger, didn't seem to want to function properly. All he knew was that Emily didn't appear to love him. As he turned away from the door, his gaze hit the full decanter of brandy. With little thought but to drown his pain until she was gone, he walked to the table and poured himself a generous measure. Dejectedly he sank into a chair before the small fire and wondered how he would face the future without her.

Delia Keaton sat on the ledge of the water fountain in the knot garden watching the remaining frogs, those who had not been large enough to escape the confines of the stone pool, swim and frolic in the water. Despite the creatures' playful antics, her thoughts were still on Emily and what she intended to do about Joshua Collins. The interview between the pair seemed to be lasting a very long time.

Looking up, she spied Sir Ethan coming from the castle towards her. Her heart danced with excitement; then she reminded herself that hers hadn't been a happy union. Why would she even consider taking such a step again, especially when Emily needed her?

"Good morning, my dear." The gentleman came and stood beside her a moment, his auburn hair looking nearly red in the morning sunlight. She gestured for him to be seated beside her on the stone ledge.

"Good morning, sir." She returned her gaze to the pool.

"What has put that frown upon your bonny face, my dear?"

Embarrassed to tell the gentleman of her thoughts of him, she avoided his intense gaze by looking out over the landscape. "I am much worried about Emily. I fear I have put her in a rather uncomfortable situation."

"How so?"

The lady twisted her handkerchief between her fingers. "I fear I was the one who informed the Collinses of Emily's return to England and her present location."

The baronet was quiet for a moment, then gave a soft

chuckle. "Did you think to protect the lovely Miss Collins from the notorious rake?"

Delia nodded her head, but couldn't bring herself to look at the gentleman. He was the earl's friend and would despise her for what she had done. But to her surprise, his strong hand reached over and grasped one of hers. A shock raced up her arm, but she allowed him to take her hand between his, even as she felt the blood pound in her ears.

"Normally I would say that would have been a wise decision, considering the lady's innocence and the gentleman's reputation, but Miss Emily Collins is special. She has touched something in Oliver that I was not certain existed."

Delia's shy gaze looked into the baronet's eyes. The feel of his warm hand on hers was making it difficult for her to think. "What do you mean?"

"I mean that Oliver Carson has fallen in love with the fair lass." He smiled at her, sensing that his words surprised her.

"Are you certain? Did he tell you he is in love with her?" Delia's fingers clutched at his hand.

"He has said nothing, but I have known him for many years. I think that from the moment you ladies arrived, I sensed Miss Collins had gotten under his skin as no woman ever had. But the night he told me he would never marry Lady Cora despite the countess's wishes, I was certain that your friend was the reason. I'm not sure he'd even realized it himself until the picnic. Did you not see the look on his face when we returned to the castle? I am certain the lass has stolen his heart."

There had been an intensity about the earl that day which Delia had never seen before, but she had thought it had to do with Lady Cora and her display of temper beside the lake. Was it possible that all her worries were for naught?

At that moment a footfall on the gravel drew her attention. She looked up to see Emily coming towards her, and the look on her face sent a chill deep into Delia's soul.

The lady came to a halt before the couple as Sir Ethan politely rose. "Pray, forgive me for interrupting your conversation with Delia, sir, but I wished to inform her that I have instructed the servants to pack our belongings. We are for London today."

The announcement surprised the pair, and they exchanged a puzzled glance. Delia knew Emily well and saw some deep emotion just below the surface of the lady's mood, but the widow instinctively sensed not to probe too much at present.

"You are leaving? Have you told Oliver?" The baronet looked from one lady to the other, his auburn brows drawn into a flat line of worry.

"Yes, I have just come from speaking with the . . . gentleman." There was a catch in the lady's voice, but she continued as if nothing unusual had occurred. "I fear I mustn't linger in Somerset a moment longer. But I do hope you will visit us once you are back in London, sir. We shall lodge several weeks at Grillon's while my solicitor makes arrangements for the purchase of a residence in Town."

Sir Ethan knew something had occurred, but he didn't have a notion what had the lady so upset. His gaze at last settled on the lovely Delia, and he said, "I shall gladly pay a visit at the first opportunity."

Delia blushed, but Emily seemed little in the mood for conversation. "Come, my dear, we must be away before nuncheon." With that Emily turned and hurried back towards the castle.

Delia offered Sir Ethan a hurried good-bye and followed her mistress.

Sir Ethan again sat on the fountain ledge, his mind searching for answers to the ladies' sudden departure. Something was afoot and he wondered what it could be. He was certain Oliver loved Emily, and the lady had shown signs of being smitten as well. Clearly something had interfered with the course of their romance. Had it been the countess and her ambitious matchmaking who'd caused a problem? Or perhaps the controlling Mr. Collins in his attempt to get Emily under his thumb?

The baronet didn't know who was the source of the interference, but he intended to set things right as much for Oliver as for himself. He knew Delia Keaton was important to him, and she would never be happy as long as Emily was miserable. Regardless of the lady's attempt at normality, he'd seen the pain in those amber eyes.

It occurred to Sir Ethan that if the ladies were leaving, then so would the Collinses. He was determined to find the truth, so he must have an interview with Joshua Collins before the gentleman departed.

The baronet's face was intense with purpose as he strode back to the castle. He gave a harsh laugh as it suddenly occurred to him that there was a certain irony to the fact that he was attempting to play Cupid when he'd failed so miserably at love himself so many years before. But when his thoughts turned to Delia, he knew that what he felt for her was far different from his momentary infatuation with his late wife. He pushed such thoughts aside. For now he must concentrate on putting Oliver and Emily's fate first.

Twelve

Some two weeks passed without Mrs. Keaton and Miss Collins hearing news from anyone who'd been at Hawk's Lair at the time of their sudden departure. Presently ensconced in comfortable rooms at Grillon's on Albemarle Street in London, they were busy making preparations for their entry into Society with visits to modistes, hatmakers and bootmakers.

Yet still they'd not ventured forth to join in the nightly revelry of the Beau Monde. Emily always seemed to have some excuse or the other which kept them from going to the opera or a play, but Delia was certain she knew the true reason. Her friend was suffering from a broken heart.

The widow was still much in the dark about what had happened that final day at the castle, since Emily refused to speak of the incident or the earl. But Delia was not fooled into believing that it was because her employer did not care for the gentleman. At times she would catch Emily with such a look of pain on her face that it wrenched the heart, only Delia was at a loss as how to help her friend, since she didn't know what was wrong.

That morning they'd risen late and were lingering over

Lynn Collum

coffee in the sitting room when a knock sounded at their door. Swarup stepped in to announce, "Sir Ethan Russell, *memsahib*. Are you in to visitors?"

Emily smiled at her friend as the widow tried to appear unaffected by the news, but Delia's eyes held a delighted glitter. "Yes, Swarup, show him up."

Within minutes the baronet strode into the room, looking handsome in his russet-brown morning coat over a tan striped waistcoat and tan pantaloons. "Good morning, Miss Collins, Mrs. Keaton. How I have missed seeing your bonny faces since you left us in Somerset."

Delia flushed pink, taking an unusual interest in the pattern of the tablecloth, as Emily rose and extended her hand to the gentleman. "We are happy to see you, sir." She hesitated but a moment, then in a small voice asked, "I hope you left all well at the castle?"

Sir Ethan, his mood buoyant, lifted the lady's hand and gallantly kissed it, but his bold gaze never deviated from Mrs. Keaton. "In truth, Miss Collins, I left no one at the castle save the servants."

Emily's brows rose in surprise. "His lordship has brought the children to Town?"

Straightening the gentleman grinned. "Why, no. In truth, 'twas their father who brought them."

Emily and Delia exchanged an elated glance at the wonderful news. The widow rose and came to rest her hand on the baronet's arm. "You mean Mr. Carson is alive and returned to England?"

"I do. He arrived from Plymouth some three nights ago, looking surprisingly hearty considering his near-fatal illness, but I would suppose several months of sea air restored his health."

Emily sighed with pleasure. "That *is* wonderful news, but why has he come to London so soon?"

"The earl, the countess—why, the whole family is returned to Town. Mr. Carson had business, but he wishes to meet you kind ladies and thank you for all you did for his children."

A look somewhere between reluctance and longing settled into Emily's amber eyes before she turned and walked to the window. "The gentleman is welcome to call at any time, Sir Ethan. We look forward to making his acquaintance."

The baronet watched Emily for a moment, then smiled as if he'd seen something that pleased him. "Well, I am certain he will write to you from Hawksworth House to request an interview once he has the children situated comfortably and his more pressing business affairs attended to."

The lady nodded her head but made no comment, returning her gaze to the traffic in the busy street.

"But I have come this morning on my own behalf to invite you bonny lasses to go for a drive in the park. 'Tis a fine day, and I have my barouche and coachman waiting."

Emily looked over her shoulder to see the look of suppressed excitement in Delia's eyes. But Emily couldn't face going out knowing the earl was once again in Town. "My dear, I insist that you go and take the air with Sir Ethan. I must stay and write a letter to my solicitor, for he is requesting that I make a decision on several financial matters."

When the widow looked as if she would decline, Sir Ethan took her hand and leaned in close to whisper, "Pray, do not say no, my dear. There are several urgent matters I would speak to you of in private." He then directed his gaze to where Emily stood, and Delia knew

at once that the matter concerned the earl and her unhappy employer.

The lady agreed and went to retrieve her bonnet and
cape. Some minutes later, as the barouche edged into
traffic on Albemarle Street, Delia eagerly asked, "What
have you learned, sir?" In her anxiety to hear news, she
placed her gloved hand on his arm.

Sir Ethan covered her hand with his as he smiled
down at her beautiful face. "My love, I have learned a
great deal. I have every hope that the affair can be set
to right. But there is a pressing matter we must settle."
Despite the open carriage and the risk of scandal, he
leaned over and kissed her willing lips. Her eager response made him smile as he drew away from her. "I
adore you, my bonny Delia. Since you left Hawk's Lair,
I have been unaccountably lonely. Will you make an old
Scotsman happy by becoming his fair bride?"

Delia blushed but gazed back into the green eyes with
devotion. "I dearly love you, my fine sir, but I cannot
leave Emily so unhappy. First you must tell me what
occurred at Hawk's Lair to make her so and how you
came to learn of it."

Sir Ethan quickly informed the lady that on the day
of their departure he'd learned nothing from the earl,
but suspecting Mr. Joshua Collins of having had a hand
in whatever had happened, he'd confronted the gentleman.

"It seems Mr. Roland Collins claims to have overheard a conversation in which Oliver plotted to ask
Emily to marry him for her money, and so Mr. Collins
repeated the conversation to your friend."

Delia looked shocked. As she withdrew her hand from
underneath Sir Ethan's, the gentleman quirked one

auburn brow at her. "Now, don't be giving me one of those looks, my love. The story was mostly a hum."

"Mostly."

"Oliver was head over heels in love with our Miss Collins long before he knew about the lady's inheritance from her uncle. Oliver only mentioned the lady's fortune to his grandmother to smooth that lady's ire at having lost Lady Cora's wealth. Believe me, Oliver cares little what Society thinks. Having fallen in love, he would have married your friend had she proven to be the governess he first thought her."

Delia smiled. "Then what shall we do to bring them together? Shall I tell her the truth of the matter?"

"I think not, for there would always be doubts. We must come up with a plan." With that the two put their heads together and began to consider how best to bring the misunderstanding to an end. At last they decided to enlist the aid of the countess, and Sir Ethan called to his coachman to return to Hawksworth House.

Back at Grillon's, Emily had watched the barouche disappear from sight with a mixture of happiness for her friend and a heavy heart that her own hopes had been dashed so cruelly. But she didn't want to think about the earl, for it hurt too much.

Certain that Sir Ethan had come to propose to her friend, Emily began to ponder what she would do for a companion after the pair wed. Propriety demanded that a single lady like herself must have a chaperon. All the single females she knew were still in Calcutta, save her cousin Bettina, but to ask that young lady to live with her would require that she reestablish contact with her uncle, and that she would not do. The simplest solution would be to hire a companion.

To Emily's surprise, Swarup was again at the door to announce a visitor. "There is a Mrs. Logan to see you, *memsahib.*"

Puzzled as to who had arrived, but happy to be distracted from her dark thoughts, she asked her servant to show the lady up. To her amazement, the sitting room door opened some minutes later to reveal her cousin Bettina, still plump but looking modish in a new traveling gown with matching bonnet topped by a yellow plume. The smile on her radiant face made her appear quite handsome.

The lady advanced across the room and took Emily's hands. "My dear cousin, I had to come to thank you and the earl for all you have done for me and my Darnell. I was certain when I begged the earl to protect you that I had chosen the right gentleman."

Emily was stunned. Here was her cousin, yet this seemed a different person from the downtrodden young woman in Somerset. This lady was babbling on in such a strange manner and full of the earl's praises, which puzzled Emily even more. "Cousin, I am most happy to see you, but I must own I don't understand what has you in such alt."

"Did the earl not tell you?"

Emily looked down at the floor. "I have not spoken to his lordship since I left Hawk's Lair."

"His solicitor found my dear curate. Not only that, but the earl has offered him the living at the local parish in Somerset. Is that not wonderful?"

Emily's head was reeling. "I fear I am somewhat at a loss. Who is this curate?"

"My husband—Darnell. We were married by special

icense last week, and my father is furious." Bettina
laughed with glee.

"I wish you joy, Cousin. But when did you ask the
earl to protect me? And what had the earl to do with
your marriage?"

Her cousin at last took note of Emily's somber mood.
Taking her by the hand, she led her to the sofa. "I begin
to think that my father created some mischief between
you and the earl, which is a great pity, for I never saw
a man more in love than Lord Hawksworth when we
had our tryst in the Long Gallery."

Emily stared at her cousin as if she'd just escaped
from Bedlam.

Bettina laughed. "Sit down, my dear. I have a great
many things to tell you."

Some thirty minutes later, after the departure of Mrs.
Logan, Emily sat with her mind in a whirl. The earl
had truly loved her long before he knew of her inheritance! Bettina had been the one to tell him she was an
heiress after he'd announced his wish to marry her.
Foolishly, she'd listened to her uncle and ruined, perhaps
forever, her chance to wed the man she loved.

Could Oliver forgive her? He was a proud man, and
she'd done all in her power to prick that pride in the
library that day. Yet even as she wondered about the
earl's forgiveness, she knew that doubts still lingered
about the conversation her cousin had overheard.

Emily suspected that too much damage had been done
for them to ever come together. She gave a deep sigh.
She'd spent the last two weeks trying to put the earl
from her mind. For her own sake, she must not begin
to engage in fanciful dreams about what might have
been. With that thought, she put aside her personal af-

fairs and drew a paper and pen to her to write her solicitor.

Oliver moved the buttered eggs around on his plate
with little interest in eating them. He'd had no appetite
since Emily had left, but he pushed the painful thoughts
of her from his mind. He had to get past the loss of
the woman he loved. Without warning, he straightened
and announced to all present, "I have decided we must
go to Yorkshire on the morrow."

The countess and James, seated across from one another, exchanged a look of anxiety. Lady Hawksworth
laid her napkin on the table. "Oliver, James has just
returned to town after an absence of nearly ten years.
Let the man at least enjoy himself a bit. Why do you
not introduce him to some of your friends?"

The earl looked up at his grandmother. "My brother
is not a stranger, madam. He has friends from before
he went to the Indies. Besides, I'm not in the mood for
going about in company."

The countess rolled her eyes at James as if to say
"do something." The younger man, having been told of
his brother's failed romance and of his grandmother's
plan to bring about a meeting of the two, said, "Oliver,
I spoke with your solicitor yesterday, as you requested,
and he was preparing several more documents for you
to sign for the transfer of Hawkland Manor to me.
Could we not remain a few more days, until all is complete? I know I have said this before, but I cannot thank
you enough—"

Oliver raised his hand. "There is no need, James. I
have intended the estate in Yorkshire for you since you

were one-and-twenty. I am merely anxious to see the
children settled into their new home."

James gave a half smile as he stared down at his
plate. " 'Tis unfortunate that I was too proud so long
ago to accept such a generous offer."

The earl rose, his face a grim mask. "Do not fret
about the past. We are all older and wiser, dear brother.
Now you must excuse me—I have business to attend
to."

As the door closed behind the earl, Lady Hawksworth
ordered, "You must send your invitation to Emily Collins at once. Time is running out."

James sighed. "I cannot like interfering in my
brother's affairs, Grandmother."

"Oh, fie, what does that matter when you will only
be helping him? What you must do is make some excuse for not being able to come to her." The lady
paused, and when her grandson made no move, she gestured with her hand. "Hurry, my boy, before your
brother again takes some notion in his head to leave
today."

James went to do as he was bidden, praying that
Oliver would forgive him for such an impertinence.

The following morning, Emily found herself with only
her newly hired maid, Ruth, on her way to Park Lane
to meet Mr. Carson. It would not have been her choice
to go to Hawksworth House, but matters had conspired
to make the earl's residence the best place for the meeting due to Delia having come down with some strange
illness which seemed to come and go at random and
Mr. Carson begging her indulgence by having her come
to him and the children.

Dressed in her new pale-green sprig-muslin gown with a dark-green velvet spencer, which had been delivered only the day before, Emily knew she looked her best. She'd taken longer than usual to get ready, always wondering if she would see the earl.

As the coach drew up in front of the elegant town house, Emily's heart raced. She was terribly torn about wanting to see Hawksworth and yet not. What if they came face-to-face and he were to reject her apology as she had so cruelly spurned his offer of marriage? She closed her eyes and tried to rally her courage to enter his home.

Pushing aside her fears, she stepped to the street and waited as the footman knocked. Minutes later, Emily was pleased when the door opened to reveal the butler.

"Miss Collins!" There was such delight in the old servant's face that her heart warmed.

" 'Tis good to see you, Bedows." She stepped in, her maid following.

"Have you come to see his lordship?" There was such a look of hope in the old man's eyes that Emily hated to disappoint him.

She shook her head. "I was invited by Mr. Carson."

Bedows seemed to realize he was forgetting his duty. He took the lady's cape, saying, "I have been instructed to put you in the Morning Room, miss. Then I shall inform Lord James and the children of your arrival."

To Emily's surprise, he led her into what she could only assume was a small private room used by the family on the ground floor instead of an upstairs drawing room. The butler promised to bring refreshments, then left her alone, her maid seated outside in the hall.

Nervous, Emily moved to the wall of windows which overlooked a large garden. Her heart leapt when, to her

urprise, she saw the earl seated in the rear of the gar-
en, apparently in deep thought, his gaze riveted on the
round. She was immediately struck by the change in
is appearance. His face looked gaunt and drawn, as if
e'd not eaten since she'd last seen him. His attire, while
roper, showed none of the meticulousness she remem-
ered. His cravat was tied in a simple knot but was
lightly askew, and his hair looked as if he'd been comb-
ng it with his fingers.

Her heart ached to see him thus, and she reached out
er hand to touch the glass as if she might reach him.
But just then she heard the door to the sitting room
pen, and her hand dropped to her side. Gathering her
vits, she turned and pasted a smile on her face.

To her surprise, it wasn't Mr. Carson standing before
er, but Lady Hawksworth. Emily suddenly wished she
adn't come. But as the lady crossed the room to her,
Emily realized that the countess had changed as well.
All the old hostility and arrogance was gone from her
ined face.

"My dear, you can have no idea how delighted I am
o see you again." The countess hugged Emily; then,
ealizing how tense the girl in her arms was, she drew
ack to look at her visitor. "Sir Ethan told me your
ncle repeated an altered version of a conversation his
on overheard at the library door."

Emily was surprised at the lady's bluntness. "And did
uch a conversation take place?"

The dowager drew Emily towards a yellow damask
ofa. "There was a conversation, but to understand what
vas said, you must let me begin at the beginning, my
lear. To do that I must go back some fifteen years to
promise Oliver made his grandfather."

The countess quickly explained how she had come to

pressure her grandson to marry to honor his old promise and how she had been the one to bring Lady Cora into the affair and Oliver's reluctance to wed at all.

"The conversation your cousin heard was about my grandson telling me that titles and money did not matter where there was love. Oliver only mentioned your fortune to overcome my foolish notions about marrying for advantage. I have promised Oliver I will no longer interfere in his affairs. Can you forgive me for having made such a mess of things?"

Emily looked down at her hands linked in a tight knot in her lap. "I can, my lady, but I think the more important question is whether the earl can forgive me."

The countess's mouth tipped into a hopeful smile. "There is but one way to find out. He is there in the garden, child. Go to him."

Emily turned to gaze at the earl, still sitting staring at the ground. Fear raced through her. What if she couldn't convince him to forgive her? So much depended on what would occur in the next few moments. She rose without further ado, going straight to the glass door and quietly letting herself into the garden.

Oliver sat on a marble bench, his mind a black void. For weeks he'd tried to convince himself he should go to Emily and try again. Sir Ethan swore to him that Mr. Collins had convinced the lady he was after her money. But Oliver knew he had only his word that it was all a lie. As the memory of her rejection played over again in his mind, he knew his pride wouldn't let him face her refusal again.

Oliver's gaze fell to a large stone mixed among the gravel. He picked it up and tossed it with all his might, as if the action might relieve some of his frustration. He'd promised not to force his attentions on Emily again. In all honesty, he wasn't certain that once he was in her presence, he could resist trying to bend her to his will by the sheer force of his passion for her. He was living a nightmare. He wanted her so badly, yet he was afraid to go to her.

The soft crunch of gravel on the walk penetrated his pain-fogged brain and he looked up. He started to his feet. "Emily!"

"My lord." Her amber eyes searched his face; then she gave a slight shrug. "There are a thousand things I should say, but I think too much talk is what got us into this predicament." She moved to stand before him. "I love you, Oliver."

The earl couldn't believe his ears. Was this a dream? He reached out his hand to stroke her cheek, and it was warm and real.

"My dearest Emily." With that he gave in to his desire and drew her into his arms and showered kisses on the lady's upturned face as she placed her arms around his neck, laughing and crying with joy as the earl again asked for her hand and she gladly gave it—along with her heart.

It was some considerable time before words were again spoken, the pair being so lost in each other, but at last Emily drew back to ask. "Should we speak of what happened?"

Oliver's arms tightened about her. "It's in the past, my love. I have only one thing to tell you to remove any doubts you may have as to my love. Your fortune is yours to do with as you wish. I shan't object if you wish to toss every last groat to the poor in the streets of London."

"Are you proposing I start a riot? For that is surely what would occur."

The earl laughed as he fingered a brown curl near her lovely face. "My dear, you may do as you please as long as you marry me."

Just then a child's voice echoed in the garden. "Miss Collins, Miss Collins, you have come to visit us!"

The earl released his hold on Emily as Honoria, Jamie, Kali, the countess, Miss Millet and James Carson entered the garden through the Yellow Morning Room.

The children dashed forward and threw themself into the lady's open arms. They were full of news of the things which had occurred since she left them, the most important of which was, naturally, the return of their father.

At last Jamie turned to Honoria and said, "See—I told you Uncle would smile again if only Miss Collins would return."

The little girl drew Emily to her. "Say you will stay with us so Uncle Oliver will smile."

Emily grinned at the earl. "I do believe I shall, my dear."

Just then the other adults arrived. First there were introductions. Then Mr. Carson, a man slightly shorter than his brother but with similar dark brown hair and blue eyes, did his best to thank the lady for all her kindness to his children.

At last the countess, too blunt to contain her curiosity, remarked, "Well, Oliver, I must assume that we are to wish you happy after having seen you maul the girl so abominably for the last several minutes."

Emily blushed, but the earl proudly put his arm round her. "Miss Collins has consented to by my wife, Grandmother."

Lady Hawksworth gave a contented sigh, then came and gave her grandson and his prospective bride a kiss. "Well, it's about time. Pray don't dawdle over the arrangements. You know how I dislike staying in Town, and I cannot leave until after the ceremony."

"I fully agree, madam." He smiled down at Emily. "What say you to a special license, my love?"

Lady Hawksworth's grey eyes grew round. "Special license! Nonsense! That will do well enough for Sir Ethan and Mrs. Keaton, but an Earl of Hawksworth does not marry in such a shabby manner. The wedding shall be in St. George's in three weeks."

Oliver shook his head. "I seem to remember something about a promise to no longer interfere in my affairs, dear lady."

The countess opened her mouth to protest; then, seeing the look on everyone's face, she begrudgingly said, "Oh, very well. I shall leave it all to you, my boy."

With that, James Carson took his grandmother's arm. "I do believe we should leave the happy couple to make their own decision. Come children, let us return indoors."

After the gentleman led his protesting children back into the town house, Oliver turned to Emily, tilting her chin up. "What say you, my love? Shall it be a grand Society affair or would you prefer something simple?"

"Well, sir, I have this amazingly beautiful Hindustani wedding dress I purchased in Calcutta." The lady then proceeded to describe the red *sari* which had so scandalized her friend.

Oliver grinned, then kissed her soundly. In a husky voice, he whispered, "You little minx, I think it must be the special license. I, and only I, shall see you in that wedding dress anon."

In the most docile of voices, Emily replied, "As ever, I am yours to command, my love."

Lord Hawksworth laughed before he kissed the managing Miss Collins soundly.

About the Author

Lynn Collum lives with her family in Florida and is the author of five Zebra Regency romances. She is currently working on a Regency trilogy focusing on two sisters and a brother. The first book in the trilogy, taking place at Christmas, will be published in December 2000, the second, taking place on Valentine's day, in February 2001 and the third, against the backdrop of a spring wedding, in April 2001. Lynn loves to hear from her readers and you may write to her at: P.O. Box 478, Deland, FL 32721. Please include a self-addressed stamped envelope if you wish a response.

<u>BOOK YOUR PLACE ON OUR WEBSITE AND MAKE THE READING CONNECTION!</u>

We've created a customized website just for our very special readers, where you can get the inside scoop on everything that's going on with Zebra, Pinnacle and Kensington books.

When you come online, you'll have the exciting opportunity to:

- View covers of upcoming books

- Read sample chapters

- Learn about our future publishing schedule (listed by publication month *and author*)

- Find out when your favorite authors will be visiting a city near you

- Search for and order backlist books from our online catalog

- Check out author bios and background information

- Send e-mail to your favorite authors

- Meet the Kensington staff online

- Join us in weekly chats with authors, readers and other guests

- Get writing guidelines

- AND MUCH MORE!

Visit our website at http://www.zebrabooks.com

Put a Little Romance in Your Life With
Fern Michaels

__Dear Emily	0-8217-5676-1	$6.99US/$8.50CAN
__Sara's Song	0-8217-5856-X	$6.99US/$8.50CAN
__Wish List	0-8217-5228-6	$6.99US/$7.99CAN
__Vegas Rich	0-8217-5594-3	$6.99US/$8.50CAN
__Vegas Heat	0-8217-5758-X	$6.99US/$8.50CAN
__Vegas Sunrise	1-55817-5983-3	$6.99US/$8.50CAN
__Whitefire	0-8217-5638-9	$6.99US/$8.50CAN

Call toll free **1-888-345-BOOK** to order by phone or use this coupon to order by mail.

Name_____

Address_____

City _____ State _____Zip_____

Please send me the books I have checked above.

I am enclosing $_____

Plus postage and handling* $_____

Sales tax (in New York and Tennessee) $_____

Total amount enclosed $_____

*Add $2.50 for the first book and $.50 for each additional book.

Send check or money order (no cash or CODs) to:

Kensington Publishing Corp., 850 Third Avenue, New York, NY 10022

Prices and Numbers subject to change without notice.

All orders subject to availability.

Check out our website at **www.kensingtonbooks.com**

More Zebra Regency Romances

__A Noble Pursuit by Sara Blayne $4.99US/$6.50CAN
    0-8217-5756-3

__Crossed Quills by Carola Dunn $4.99US/$6.50CAN
    0-8217-6007-6

__A Poet's Kiss by Valerie King $4.99US/$6.50CAN
    0-8217-5789-X

__Exquisite by Joan Overfield $5.99US/$7.50CAN
    0-8217-5894-2

__The Reluctant Lord by Teresa Desjardien $4.99US/$6.50CAN
    0-8217-5646-X

__A Dangerous Affair by Mona Gedney $4.50US/$5.50CAN
    0-8217-5294-4

__Love's Masquerade by Violet Hamilton $4.99US/$6.50CAN
    0-8217-5409-2

__Rake's Gambit by Meg-Lynn Roberts $4.99US/$6.50CAN
    0-8217-5687-7

__Cupid's Challenge by Jeanne Savery $4.50US/$5.50CAN
    0-8217-5240-5

__A Deceptive Bequest by Olivia Sumner $4.50US/$5.50CAN
    0-8217-5380-0

__A Taste for Love by Donna Bell $4.99US/$6.50CAN
    0-8217-6104-8

Call toll free **1-888-345-BOOK** to order by phone or use this coupon to order by mail.

Name_____

Address_____

City _____ State _____Zip_____

Please send me the books I have checked above.

I am enclosing $_____

Plus postage and handling* $_____

Sales tax (in New York and Tennessee only) $_____

Total amount enclosed $_____

*Add $2.50 for the first book and $.50 for each additional book.

Send check or money order (no cash or CODs) to:

Kensington Publishing Corp., 850 Third Avenue, New York, NY 10022

Prices and Numbers subject to change without notice.

All orders subject to availability.

Check out our website at **www.kensingtonbooks.com**